Oliver Optic

The Boat Club

Or, the Bunkers of Rippleton

Oliver Optic

The Boat Club
Or, the Bunkers of Rippleton

ISBN/EAN: 9783337413224

Printed in Europe, USA, Canada, Australia, Japan

Cover: Foto ©Andreas Hilbeck / pixelio.de

More available books at **www.hansebooks.com**

THE

BOAT CLUB;

OR,

THE BUNKERS OF RIPPLETON.

A Tale for Boys.

OLIVER OPTIC.

CINCINNATI:
RICKEY, MALLORY & CO.
BOSTON: CROSBY, NICHOLS, LEE & CO.
NEW YORK: PHINNEY, BLAKEMAN & MASON.
1861.

STEREOTYPED AT THE
BOSTON STEREOTYPE FOUNDRY.

TO

MY NEPHEW,

William Parker Jewett,

THIS BOOK

IS AFFECTIONATELY DEDICATED.

PREFACE.

THE author of the following story pleads guilty of being more than half a boy himself; and in writing a book to meet the wants and the tastes of " Young America," he has had no difficulty in stepping back over the weary waste of years that separates youth from maturity, and entering fully into the spirit of the scenes he describes. He has endeavored to combine healthy moral lessons with a sufficient amount of exciting interest to render the

1 *

story attractive to the young; and he hopes he has not mingled these elements of a good juvenile book in disproportionate quantities.

DORCHESTER, Sept. 20, 1854.

CONTENTS.

8 CONTENTS.

THE BOAT CLUB.

THE BOAT CLUB;

OR,

𝕿𝖍𝖊 𝕭𝖚𝖓𝖐𝖊𝖗𝖘 𝖔𝖋 𝕽𝖎𝖕𝖕𝖑𝖊𝖙𝖔𝖓.

CHAPTER I.

FRANK SEDLEY.

"How much have you got, Frank?" asked Charles Hardy of his friend, Frank Sedley.

"Four dollars and seventy-five cents."

"That is more than twice as much as I have. Won't you have a glorious time?"

It was the evening of the third of July, and the two boys were counting the money they had saved for Independence. Captain Sedley, the father of Frank, had promised to carry him and his friend to Boston to attend the celebration, and they had long

looked forward to the event with the liveliest antici-
pations of pleasure.

"I don't know, Charley," replied Frank Sedley,
as he slid the money into the purse; "I was thinking of something else."

"What, Frank?"

"I was thinking how poor the widow Weston is,
and how much good this money I am going to throw
away in fire crackers and gingerbread would do
her."

"Perhaps it would."

"I know it would."

"But you are not going to spoil our fun by giving
it to her, are you?"

"There are a great many boys who will have no
money to spend to-morrow — Tony Weston, for in-
stance," continued Frank.

"Tony is a good fellow."

"That he is; and his mother has a terrible hard
time of it to support him and his sister."

"I suppose she has. Why don't you ask your
father to help her?"

"He does help her. He gives her wood, and

flour, and a great many other things; and my mother employs her to do sewing. She is willing to work."

" And Tony works too."

" He is too young to do much; but he loves his mother, and tries to do all he can to lighten her burden."

" He makes a dollar a week, sometimes."

" I was thinking just now that I would give Mrs. Weston the money I had saved for Independence."

" Pooh! Frank."

" It would do her a great deal of good."

" What is the use of going to Boston, if you have no money?" asked Charles, who was not a little disturbed by this proposed disbursement of the fourth of July funds.

" I can stay at home, then."

" That wouldn't be fair, Frank."

" Why not?"

" You not only rob yourself of the fun, but me too."

" I really pity the poor woman so much that I cannot find it in my heart to spend the money

2

foolishly, when it will buy so many comforts for her."

" Your father will give you some money for her."

" That isn't the thing,"

" What do you mean ? "

" You went to meeting last Sunday ? "

" Yes."

" And heard the sermon ? "

" Some of it," replied Charles, smiling.

" You remember the minister spoke of the luxury of doing good; of the benefit one gets by sacrificing his inclination for the good of others, or something like that; I can't express it as he did, though I have the idea."

Frank paused, and looked earnestly into the face of his friend to ascertain whether he was likely to find any sympathy in his heart.

" I do remember it, Frank. He told a story to illustrate his meaning."

" That was it. I don't very often mind much about the sermon but somehow I was very much interested in that one."

" And so you mean to give your money to the

widow Weston, just to see how you will feel after it," added Charles, with a laugh

" No ; that isn't it."

" What is it, then ? "

" I give it to her because I really feel that she needs it more than I do. I feel a pleasure in the thought of sacrificing my inclination for her happiness, which is more satisfactory than all the fun I anticipate to-morrow."

" You'll be a parson, Frank."

" No, I won't; I will do my duty."

" Have you made up your mind ? "

" We can have a good time at home."

" Pooh ! "

" I shall give my money to the widow Weston at any rate."

Charles Hardy could not but admire the generosity of his friend ; though he found it difficult to abandon the thought of the pleasure he anticipated in spending the fourth in Boston. He stood in silent thought a few moments, and then spoke.

" Well, Frank," said he, " if you have determined to give your money to the widow, I shall follow your example."

" But, Charley, I didn't mean to influence you. 1 will even go to Boston with you, though I have no money."

"I will give my money to the widow. I think you are right."

"Good, Charley! I like you for it."

"I have two dollars and a quarter," continued Charles, taking the money from his pocket.

"We shall make up just seven dollars. How it will rejoice the heart of the poor woman!" exclaimed Frank, with enthusiasm.

" So it will. But don't you think your father will make it up to you, when he finds out how generous we have been ? "

Frank looked into the face of his companion with an expression of painful surprise on his countenance.

"I don't want him to do so."

" Why not ? "

" It would rob the action of all its merit. If you give your money with the hope of having it restored to you, I beg you not to give it at all. I have abandoned all thoughts of having any money to spend to-morrow."

" And not go to Boston ? "

" No."

" What will your father say, when you tell him you are not going? He will want to know the reason."

" I will tell him day after to-morrow."

" He will want to know to-morrow."

" I can persuade him to wait. Shall we go over to-night, and give the money to Mrs. Weston ? "

" Yes, if you like."

" Wait a moment, and I will go into the house, and ask my father to let me stay out till nine o'clock."

Frank bounded lightly over the green lawn to his father's house, near which the conversation took place.

Rippleton, the scene of my story, is a New England village, situated about ten miles from Boston. It is one of those thriving places which have sprung into existence in a moment, as it were, before the potent stimulus of a railroad and a water privilege. Twenty years ago, it consisted of only one factory and about a dozen houses. Now, it is a great, bustling village, and probably in a few years will become a city. Trains of cars arrive and depart every hour, as the Traveller's Guide says; and a double row of factories extends along the sides of the river. It has its banks, its great hotels, its dozen churches, and its noisy streets — indeed, almost all the pomp and circumstance of a great city.

About a mile from the village was the beautiful residence of Captain Sedley — Frank's father. He was a retired shipmaster, in which capacity he had acquired a handsome fortune. His house was built within a few rods of Wood Lake — a beautiful sheet of water, nearly three miles in length, and a little more than a mile in width. On the river which formed the outlet of this lake, the village of Rippleton was situated, and its clear waters turned the great wheels of the factories.

Captain Sedley had chosen this place in which to spend the evening of his days, because it seemed to him the loveliest spot in all New England. The glassy, transparent lake, with its wood-crowned shores, its picturesque rocks, its little green islands, indeed, every thing about it, was so grand and beautiful that it seemed more like the creation of a pure and enthusiastic imagination than a substantial reality. The retired shipmaster loved the beautiful in nature, and his first view of the silver lake and the surrounding country enabled him to decide that this spot should be his future habitation. He bought the land, built him a fine house, and was as happy as a mortal could desire to be.

But I beg my young reader not to think that Captain Sedley was happy because he lived in such a beautiful place, and had such a fine house, and so much money at his command; for a beautiful prospect, a costly dwelling, and plenty of money, alone, cannot make a person contented and happy. The richest men are often the most miserable; a bed of down may be a bed of thorns; and a magnificent mansion will not keep out the fiends of remorse.

Captain Sedley was a good man. He had always endeavored to be true to his God, and true to himself; to be just and righteous towards his fellowmen. In an active business experience of twenty years, he had found a great many opportunities of doing good — opportunities which he had had the moral courage to improve. He loved his God by loving his fellow-man. He had made his fortune by being honest and just. He had lived a good life ; and, as every good man will, whether he get rich or poor by it, he was receiving his reward in the serene happiness of his days in this world, and in the cherished hope of everlasting bliss in the world to come.

Captain Sedley was happy, too, in his family. Mrs. Sedley was an amiable and devoted woman, and Frank, his only child, was an affectionate and obedient son. Perhaps my young friends cannot fully appreciate the amount of satisfaction which a parent derives from the good character of the child. Though the worthy shipmaster had a beautiful estate and plenty of money, if his son had been a liar, a thief, a profane swearer, — in short, if Frank had been a bad boy, — he could not have been happy. If a wise and good father could choose between having his son a hopeless drunkard or villain, and laying his cold form in the dark grave, never more to see him on earth, he would no doubt choose the latter. Almost all parents say so. and their words are so

earnest, their tears so eloquent, that we cannot but
believe it. Such was the father of Frank Sedley,
and it was such a father that made so good a son.

Charles Hardy was the son of one of the factory
agents, who was Captain Sedley's nearest neighbor.
and a strong friendship had grown up between the
two boys. Charles's character was essentially different from that of his friend ; but as I prefer that my
young reader should judge his disposition for himself, and distinguish between the good and the evil
of his thoughts and actions as the story proceeds, I
shall not now tell him what kind of a boy he was.

CHAPTER II.

WIDOW WESTON.

NEAR the house of Captain Sedley, a sandy beach extended from the road, which wound along the margin of the lake, down to the water's side. It was here that Charles Hardy waited the return of his friend. He was thinking of the sacrifice they had concluded to make for the widow Weston; and it must be confessed that he felt a little sad at the thought of resigning all the fine things they had projected in connection with their excursion to the city.

On the water, secured by a pole driven into the sand, floated a raft which some of the boys in the neighborhood had built, and with which they amused themselves in paddling about the lake. It was a rude structure, made by lashing together four rails in the form of a square, and placing planks across the upper side of them. The boys who had constructed it lived farther down the lake in the direction of the village. They did not bear a very good character in the neighborhood. If an orchard was robbed, a henroost plundered, or any other mischief done in the vicinity, it could generally be traced to them. They always played together, went and came from school together, planned and executed their mischief together, so that they came to be regarded as a unit of roguery, and people never saw one of them without wondering where the rest were.

The foremost of these unruly fellows was Tim Bunker. He was the ruling spirit of their party, and had the reputation of being a notoriously bad boy. He would lie, swear, cheat, and steal; and people, judging his followers by their ringleader, at last got into the way of calling them the Bunkers.

Of course, Captain Sedley was unwilling that his son should associate with such boys as the Bunkers; but so much did Frank dislike their company, that it was scarcely necessary to caution him to avoid them.

While Charles Hardy was waiting, he walked down to the water's edge. The sun was just sinking behind the green hills in the west, reflecting the shadows of the beautiful gold and purple clouds upon the bosom of the silver lake. A gentle breeze was blowing down the valley, and the little waves broke with a musical ripple upon the pebbly sands. It was a lovely hour and a lovely scene; and Charles felt the sweet influence of both. He looked out upon the lake, and wished he was floating over its tiny wavelets.

He stepped upon the raft, and thought how pleasant and how exciting it would be to sail over to Centre Isle, as the little wood-crowned islet, that rose from the middle of the lake, was called. Pulling up the stake that held the raft, he pushed out a little way from the shore. The sensation which the motion of the raft produced was new and strange to him, and he felt a longing desire to sail farther. But, just then, Frank returned.

"My father is not at home," said he.

"Can't you go, then?" asked Charles, as he pushed the raft to the shore again.

"Yes; I told my mother where I was going."

"Frank, let us go up to Mrs. Weston's on this raft. She lives close by the shore of the lake."

"My father told me never to go on the lake without permission from him."

"Pooh! What harm can there be in it?"

"I don't know as any."

"Let us go then."

"My father told me not to go on the lake."

"But he has gone away, you said."

"I cannot disobey him."

"He never will know it"

"You don't mean what you say, Charley. You would not have me go directly contrary to what my father has told me, just because he is not here to see me."

Charles felt a little ashamed, and replacing the stake that secured the raft, jumped on shore.

"It is such a delightful evening, and it would be so pleasant to take a little sail!" said he.

"I don't think that raft is very safe. I saw the Bunkers on it the other day, and they stood knee deep in water."

"I am not afraid of it."

"No matter; my father told me not to go on the

lake, which is quite reason enough for me not to do so."

" But the Bunkers seem to have a first-rate time on it."

" Perhaps they do."

" But we fellows that have to mind what our fathers and mothers tell us are the losers by our obedience."

Frank smiled ; he could not help doing so at the thought of one who had just been counselling him to disobedience making such a remark.

" I am quite sure I am contented."

" But don't you think the Bunkers have more fun than we do ?   Tim Bunker don't care any more about what his father says than he does about the fifth wheel of a coach, and he always seems to have a first-rate time."

" Appearances are deceitful," replied Frank, with a sage smile.   " Do you think we should enjoy our-selves sailing on that raft up to our knees in water ? "

" The water wouldn't hurt us."

" Not so much as the disobedience, it is true ; but I don't care much about such fun as that."

"Tim Bunker asked me to sail with him over to the island, yesterday, and I had a great mind to go. If it had been any other fellow, I would."

"Your father told you not to go on the lake."

"He never would have known it."

"Perhaps not; but you would not have felt any better on that account."

"For my part, I hate to be tied to my mother's apron string when there is any fun going on. I don't see why we shouldn't have a good time once in a while, as well as the Bunkers, who are no better than we are."

"I don't know how it is with you; but I can enjoy myself enough, and obey my parents at the same time."

"Right, Frank!" exclaimed Captain Sedley, who at this moment stepped down from the grove adjoining the beach, where he had overheard a part of the conversation. "So you think, Charles, that the boys who disobey their parents enjoy themselves most."

"No, sir. I don't exactly mean that; but the Bunkers have some first-rate times with this raft," replied Charles, very much confused by the sudden appearance of Frank's father.

" But their lives are continually in danger," added Captain Sedley.

" O, sir, they can all swim."

" All of them ? "

" Like ducks, sir."

" Suppose one of them should fall overboard half a mile from the land, where I saw them yesterday. Do you think he could swim ashore ? "

" Tim could."

" There are a great many things to be considered in such an attempt. His clothes might encumber him ; he might have the cramp ; he might get frightened."

" The others could save him."

" We do not know what they could do. Boys at play are very different from boys in the hour of peril. When I was a sailor before the mast, one of my shipmates, a very expert swimmer ordinarily, fell from the mainyard arm into the sea. Two of us jumped in to assist him, but he sank to the bottom like a lump of lead, and we never saw him again."

" That was strange," added Charles.

" He was taken unawares ; he lost his self-command, and it might be so with the Bunkers. This rafting is dangerous business, and I advise you never to engage in it ; " and Captain Sedley walked off towards his house.

" Father, I want to go up to the widow Weston's a little while," said Frank.

" Very well ; but you must be back so as to go to bed and get up in season for your excursion to the city to-morrow."

" Come, Charley, I guess we won't go up on the raft," said Frank, with a pleasant laugh.

" I guess not ; " and the two boys trotted off towards the poor cottage of the widow Weston.

It was situated near the lake, about half a mile from Captain Sedley's. Mrs. Weston was the widow of a poor laboring man who had died about a year before our story opens. She was the mother of four children — three sons and a daughter. Her oldest son, who was now twenty-two years old, had been in California nearly two years, having left his home a year before the death of his father. She had

3 *

received one letter from him on his arrival at San Francisco, since which she had heard nothing of him, and had long since given up all hopes of ever seeing him again. She had not a doubt but that he had found a grave in the golden soil of that far-off land. She mourned him as dead; and all the earthly hopes of the poor mother were concentrated in her remaining children.

Anthony, the next son, whom every body called Tony, was now thirteen years old. He was an active, industrious boy, and all the neighbors were willing to employ him on their farms and about their houses, so that he was able to do a great deal towards supporting the family. He was a good boy, so honest and truthful, so kind-hearted, and so devoted to his poor mother, that he was a great favorite in the vicinity, and some of the richer folks, when they really had no work for him, would find something for him to do; for he was so proud and high-spirited that he would not take money that he had not earned.

Mary Weston, the daughter, was eleven years of age. Like her brother, she had a sweet and gentle disposition, and did all she could to assist her poor mother in the strait of her poverty. But Mrs. Weston, though she had a hard struggle to get along, sent her daughter to school winter and summer, preferring to deprive herself of many of the comforts of life rather than have her daughter forego the advantages of a tolerable education. Mary, though her little hands were too feeble to work much, felt that she was a burden to her toiling, self-denying parent, and though she could not persuade her to let her stay at home and help her, used all her time out of school in taking care of little Richard, then only three years old. By constantly striving to be useful, and by continually watching for opportunities to be of service to her mother, she very sensibly diminished the burdens of her cares.

Poor as the widow Weston was, hard as she was obliged to struggle for a subsistence, she was happy, and her children were happy. They had no fine house, no money, no rich carpets, no beds of down, as their rich neighbor had, yet they were quite as happy as he was. The God of nature gave them the same beautiful prospect of lake, and hills, and woods, and rocks to look out upon, and if these things helped to gladden their hearts, it was goodness which lay at the foundation of all their joys, which cast a ray of sunshine across the path of poverty and want. They were contented with their lot, hard and bitter as many others deemed it, and contentment made them happy — prepared their hearts to enjoy the blessings of plenty, if God, in his mercy, should ever bestow it upon them.

The boys found the family at supper, and Frank could not but contrast his evening meal with that of the poor widow's family. He had just had the choicest fruits, nice cake, hot waffles and muffins, set before him; they had only brown bread and very white butter. He had used silver dishes and silver forks; they ate their coarse fare from a few half broken plates. His father was rich, and they were very poor.

"You are welcome, Master Frank; I am glad to see you, and Master Charles too," said Mrs. Weston, rising from the table and handing them chairs. "I hope your father and mother are well."

"Very well, I thank you, ma'am," replied Frank.

"I have called to see you about something, and I want to see you alone," added he, in a low tone, for he did not want Tony, who was a great deal prouder than his mother, to know the nature of his errand.

Just then Tony finished his supper, and Mrs. Weston sent him out to feed the hens.

"I have brought you a present, Mrs. Weston," continued Frank; "I hope you will accept it."

"Indeed, Master Frank, you are always very good to me ; and your father and mother too," replied the widow.

"Here are seven dollars. Charles and I wish to give you this sum."

"Seven dollars!" exclaimed the widow; for to a poor woman like her this was a very large sum.

"Charles and I had saved it for the fourth of July ; but we thought how much good it would do you, who have to work so hard, and we determined to make you a present of it."

"May God bless you both!" exclaimed the widow, wiping a tear of gratitude from her eye; "but I cannot think of taking your money."

"But, Mrs. Weston, you *must* take it."

" And you give up your pleasure for a poor body like me ? "

" We give the money to you because it will afford us a greater pleasure than to spend it."

" How noble and generous ! but you wrong yourselves."

" O, no, we don't," said Charles ; and at that moment he felt happier than if all the gingerbread and fire crackers in the world had been showered down upon him.

" Hush ! here comes Tony. Not a word to him about it, if you please."

" Heaven bless you, boys ! " said the poor woman as she put the money in her pocket.

Frank and Charles talked a few moments with Tony about the " glorious fourth," and then took leave of the family.

CHAPTER III.

CHARLES HARDY.

CAPTAIN SEDLEY was an early riser. Every morning at sunrise he was abroad in the pleasant grove
that bordered the lake near his house. It was a
favorite spot, and he had spent a great deal of time
and money in bringing Art into communion with
Nature in his lovely retreat. He had cleared out
the underbrush, made gravel walks and avenues
through it, erected a summer house in the valley,
and an observatory on the summit of the hill, which
terminated on the lake side in a steep, rocky preci-
pice, at whose base the waters rippled.

The worthy shipmaster was a devout man, which
was perhaps the reason why he so much enjoyed his
morning walk. It was the pleasantest hour of all
the day to him ; a fit time for meditation and for
the contemplation of the gorgeous scenery that surrounded his habitation. The trees looked greener,

and the lake more limpid then, when his mind was invigorated by the peaceful slumbers of the preceding night; and there, in his favorite retreat, while all nature was smiling upon him, went up his morning orison to that beneficent Being who had spared him yet another day, and crowned his life with loving kindness and tender mercies.

It was the morning of the fourth of July, and the sounds of the booming cannon and the pealing bells, which the westerly breeze bore up the lake, reminded him of the gratitude he owed to God for the political, social, and religious privileges which had been bequeathed to the country by the fathers of the revolution. He prayed for his country, that a blessing might always rest upon it.

As he walked along, thus engaged in his inaudible devotions, he heard a footstep behind him. The solitude of his morning walk was seldom disturbed by the intrusion of others. Turning, he recognized the friend of his son.

" You are abroad early, Charles," said he.

" Yes, sir ; this is the fourth of July."

" And you feel like a little patriot on the occasion."

" I feel like having some fun."

" No doubt of it ; I am afraid the boys think more of the smoke and noise of the day than they do of the momentous event it commemorates."

" We like to have a good time, and the fourth of July comes but once a year."

" Probably you will be fully satisfied before night comes."

" I don't know," replied Charles, in a tone and with an expression of countenance which attracted the attention of Captain Sedley.

" You don't know ! I thought you were depending upon a good time in the city ! "

" We *did* anticipate a great deal of pleasure ; but we have given it up."

" Indeed ! I have made preparations to take you to Boston."

" We have given it up, sir," repeated Charles.

" Frank ? "

" Yes, sir."

" He has not mentioned the fact to me."

" But he intends to do so."

4

"What is the meaning of all this? I am surprised."

"I knew you would be," said Charles, evasively.

"But why have you given it up?"

"O, that's a secret."

"Is it, indeed? Then you really are not going?"

"No, sir."

"I suppose the secret is not to be divulged to me."

"No, sir."

Captain Sedley was not a little perplexed by what he heard. The proposed excursion had been the topic of conversation for the last fortnight, and Charles and Frank had both manifested the liveliest interest in it. And now, that the whole scheme had been abandoned, the anticipated pleasure voluntarily resigned, was strange and incomprehensible. At first he was disposed to believe some more agreeable plan of spending the day had been devised, and it seemed questionable to him whether the plan which must be kept secret could meet his approbation.

"It was Frank's notion, Mr. Sedley."

"And you have promised not to tell me?"

"O, no, sir; I don't know as Frank would like it if I should do so, though I can't see what harm it would do."

"Of course, you must do as you think proper," replied Captain Sedley. "I don't wish you to betray Frank's confidence, unless you think he is doing wrong."

"Nothing wrong, sir."

"Then why should it be kept secret?"

"I do not know of any reason why it should. You won't tell Frank if I let the cat out of the bag?" said Charles, with a kind of forced laugh.

"Certainly not, if you wish it."

"Well, then, we are not going because we have no money to spend."

"No money! Why, I gave Frank three dollars towards it no longer ago than yesterday, and he had some before that," replied Captain Sedley, not a little alarmed at the revelation.

"Frank had four dollars and seventy-five cents, and I had two dollars and twenty-five cents, which made seven dollars between us."

"What have you done with it?" asked the kind father, fearful lest his son had been doing wrong.

"Last night we concluded to give our money to the widow Weston, instead of spending it for candy and crackers, and stay at home instead of going to Boston."

An expression of pleasure lighted up the features of the devoted father. The confession of Charles was a great relief to him.

"Well done, boys!" exclaimed he. "That was noble and generous," and involuntarily he thrust his hand into his pocket, and drew forth his purse.

"Frank proposed it," said Charles, a gleam of satisfaction lighting up his eye as he beheld the purse.

Captain Sedley held it in his hand a moment, looked searchingly at Charles, and then returned it to his pocket.

"It was a noble deed, Charles, and I had rather hear such a thing of my son than to have all the wealth and honors which the world can give, bestowed upon him."

Charles looked disappointed when he saw Captain Sedley restore his purse to his pocket again.

"And Frank means to keep it a secret, does he?" continued the delighted father.

"Yes, sir; till to-morrow."

"Very well; I will not mention the fact that **you** have told me about it."

"Thank you, sir," replied Charles, doubtfully.

"And I am glad you told me — that is, if you have not betrayed his confidence;" and Captain Sedley looked rather sharply at Charles.

"O, no, sir; I have not."

"Because, when he tells me he does not intend to go, I should otherwise have insisted on knowing the reason."

Charles was already sorry he had said a word about it.

"It was a noble sacrifice, Charles," continued Captain Sedley, with much enthusiasm. "If *from a worthy motive* we sacrifice our inclinations for the good of others, we are always sure of finding our reward -- indeed, the act is its own reward."

4*

Charles began to feel a little uneasy. It seemed to him as though Captain Sedley never looked so sharply at him before. What could he mean? He had given all his money to the widow Weston as well as Frank; but Captain Sedley's looks seemed to reprove rather than commend him. He did not feel satisfied with himself, or with Captain Sedley — why, he could not exactly tell; so he happened to think that his father might want him, and ran home as fast as his legs would carry him.

But his father did not want him, and he walked nervously about the house till breakfast time. He had no appetite, and every thing seemed to go wrong with him.

"Come, Charles," said his mother, "eat your breakfast, or you will get hungry before you get to Boston."

"Ain't a going," answered he, sulkily.

"Why not?" asked his father and mother, in the same breath.

"Haven't got any money."

"No money! Where are the two dollars I

gave you yesterday?" asked Mr. Hardy, rather sternly.

" Gave them away."

" You did ? "

" Yes, sir."

" To whom ? "

" Frank proposed last night to give our money to the widow Weston, instead of spending it; and like a great fool, as I was, I agreed to it."

" Poor fellow! It was too bad!" added Mrs. Hardy.

" What did he do it for, then ? " said Mr. Hardy.

" Of course, he didn't want to be behind Frank n doing a good action."

" But he is a long way behind him."

" Why, husband ! "

" He has given the woman the money and played the hypocrite," replied Mr. Hardy, with the most evident expression of disgust in his tones and looks, " just like a great many folks who put money into the contribution box for missions and Bible societies, because they think it looks well."

"But, husband, you will give him some more money? You will make up the sum to him which he has given in charity?"

"Given in charity! Given in hypocrisy, you mean! I shall do no such thing."

"Deprive the poor boy of all his anticipated pleasure?" said the indulgent mother.

"The bitter fruit of his own hypocrisy," replied Mr. Hardy.

"You are too bad!"

"No, I am not. If he gave away his money because he thought it was an act of charity, that would look well; that would make Frank and his father think better of him; he is rightly served, and I am disposed to shut him up in this room with a good book to teach him better, instead of letting him go to the celebration."

Mr. Hardy was a blunt, honest man; perhaps a little too much inclined to be harsh with his son when he had done wrong. Perhaps his views of parental discipline were not altogether correct; but in the main he meant right. He was disgusted at the conduct of Charles, and thought no penalty too severe to atone for it.

"On the other hand," continued he, "if he had made up his mind to sacrifice his inclination at the call of charity, he would not have felt as he does now. He would have been contented to stay at home. He would have found a nobler satisfaction in the consciousness of having done a good deed, than in all the anticipated pleasures of the celebration. It is very plain to me the whole thing was an act of gross hypocrisy;" and Mr. Hardy rose from the table, and left the room.

Charles understood his father's analysis of his conduct. He felt that it was truthful. What would his father have said if he had known his motive in seeking Captain Sedley that morning? He was ashamed of himself, and was glad that his father knew nothing about it.

He had not yet lost all hope that Captain Sedley would reimburse the sums they had given the widow, and take them to Boston. But Frank's father, appreciating the noble sacrifice his son had made, was

content that he should receive all the moral discipline to be derived from the act.   Therefore he said
nothing about it, and went to the city alone.

.Charles waited impatiently till ten o'clock; but no
one came for him, and he left the house in search of
such enjoyment as Rippleton could afford him.

CHAPTER IV.

FOURTH OF JULY.

CHARLES HARDY was sadly disappointed. He had given his money to the widow Weston in the fullest confidence that it would be refunded to him, and that he should be able to attend the celebration in Boston. When Frank had proposed the charitable plan, his heart told him how good and pleasant it would be to assist the poor woman. His feelings were with him in the benevolent design — it was a mere impulse, however, which prompted him to join in the act. He thought of the sacrifice, but the hope of not being actually compelled to make it, in the end, involuntarily helped him to a decision.

His father had misjudged his motive in calling him hypocritical; for he really felt like doing the noble deed. He felt kindly towards the widow Weston; but his *principle* was not strong and deep enough to enable him to bear the deprivation which his benevolent act had laid upon him, with pleasure, or even with a good grace.

It was not so with Frank. He had given without the hope of reward, and in staying at home on the fourth of July, he was perfectly contented, because it was the price he paid for the pleasure of doing good.

Charles, when he found that Captain Sedley did not come for him, hastened over to find Frank. He and Tony Weston were on the beach.

"Hollo, Charley! We have been waiting for you," said Frank, as he approached.

"Hollo, fellows! What's in the wind?" replied Charles. "What are you going to do to-day?"

"We were just thinking about something."

"Has your father gone to the city, Frank?"

"Yes."

"What did he say?"

"Nothing."

"Didn't he look surprised?"

"Not much. He only asked me the reason, and I said I would tell him to-morrow. He didn't say any more about it. Got off slick, didn't I?"

"First rate."

"What are you talking about?" asked Tony, to whom, of course, this conversation was unintelligible.

"Tell you some other time, Tony," replied Charles. "Now what shall we do to-day?"

"I don't know; here comes Uncle Ben; perhaps he can give us an idea."

Uncle Ben was an old seaman, who had sailed a great many years in the employ of Captain Sedley. He was a rough, blunt old fellow, but so honest, warm-hearted, and devoted to his employer, that when the latter retired from the duties of his profession, he had given him a home on his estate. Uncle Ben was a good sailor; but he had never risen above the place of second mate. Without much ambition to distinguish himself, or to make money, he was perfectly content to follow the fortunes of Captain Sedley, even in an humble capacity.

Frank was an especial favorite of Uncle Ben, and as the old sailor's habits were good, and as his ideas of morality and religion rendered him a safe companion for his son, Captain Sedley had permitted and encouraged their intimacy. During the long winter evenings, he listened with the most intense interest and delight to Uncle Ben's descriptions of sea life, and of the various countries he had visited.

With the neighbors, and especially the boys in the vicinity, the old sailor was respected and treated with a great deal of consideration. He was an old man, but he had always maintained an unblemished character. He was full of kindness and sympathy, always manifesting the liveliest regard for the welfare of his friends; and on this account people had got into the way of calling him by the familiar *sobriquet* of Uncle Ben. It is true he was sometimes rude and rough, but his kind heart atoned for the blemishes in his deportment.

Though Captain Sedley considered Uncle Ben a necessary appendage to his estate, he did not impose upon him the performance of any very arduous duties. He kept a pleasure boat on the lake, and the old sailor had the entire charge of that. Occasionally he worked a little in the garden, groomed the horses, and did the " chores " about the house ; but, to use his own expression, he was " laid up in ordinary."

"Here comes Uncle Ben," said Frank, as the veteran approached them.

"I have been lookin' for you, boys. What are you up to here?"

"Nothing, Uncle Ben."

"What do you stand there for, then? Arn't this the fourth of July?"

"It is, Uncle Ben; and we were thinking what we should do with ourselves. Can't you tell us?"

"That I can, boys; I am goin' over across the lake in the boat, and Cap'n Sedley told me I might take you over with me, if you'd like to go."

"Hurrah!" cried Charles Hardy, throwing up his cap with delight.

"That we will, Uncle Ben, and right glad we are of the chance to go," replied Frank.

"Tumble up to the boat house, then," replied Uncle Ben, as he hobbled after the boys, who, delighted with the prospect of a sail on the lake, bounded off like so many antelopes.

The boat was loosened from her moorings in the boat house, and the boys jumped in.

" You will let me steer, won't you, Uncle Ben?
said Frank.

" Sartin, if you want to.   Take the helm."

The old sailor hoisted the sails, and the boat stood
out towards the middle of the lake.

" Steady, there," said Uncle Ben ; " keep the
sails full."

Frank found it was not so easy a matter even to
steer a sailboat as he had anticipated ; for one moment he stopped the boat by " throwing her up into
the wind," and the next ran her almost on shore by
" keeping away."

" Keep her away ! " cried Uncle Ben.   " That will
do ; steady as she is.   No, no ; you are six p'ints
out of course now.   Luff a little !   Hard a port ! "

" I don't know what you mean, Uncle Ben ; I
think you had better steer yourself," said Frank, resigning the helm.   .

" I think I had."

Under the old sailor's skilful management, the
boat soon reached Centre Isle, where they decided to
land.

" Now, boys, if you want to celebrate a little,

here are half a dozen bunches of crackers," said Uncle Ben, as he took a little package from the locker in the stern of the boat.

"Bravo, Uncle Ben! We will have a nice time."

"Now, if you are a mind to stay here and have a good time, while I sail over to the other shore to see a sick man, I will give you a good sail when I return."

"Hurrah! we will, Uncle Ben. Have you got any matches?"

"There are matches and a slowmatch in the bundle," replied Uncle Ben, as he pushed off. "Now, blaze away, and don't burn your fingers."

"Now for it!" exclaimed Charles, as he lighted the slowmatch. "Here goes the first shot. Hurrah!"

The boys were in high glee. The crackers snapped admirably, and the little forest of Centre Isle reverberated with the reports of their mimic guns. Various expedients were devised to vary the entertainment. Crackers were fired in the water, in the stumps, thrown in the air, or half buried in the wet sand of the beach.

"By gracious! the Bunkers are coming!" ex-

5 *

claimed Tony Weston, as he discerned the raft, navigated by half a dozen boys, approaching the island.

" Let them come," said Charles.

" I had rather they would not come," added Frank.

" What harm will they do ? "

" They are quarrelsome and disagreeable."

" Well, they won't be here this half hour yet; that is one consolation; and we can have a good time till they do get here," returned Charles, as he lighted a whole bunch of the crackers.

" Go it ! " cried Tony. " Hurrah ! Fourth of July comes but once a year."

" Don't fire them all at once, Charley," interposed Frank.

" That is all the fun of it."

" But the fun won't last long at that rate."

" We must fire them all before the Bunkers get here, or they will take them away from us."

And before the half hour which Charles had given them to reach the island had expired, their stock was entirely gone, their ammunition exhausted, their noisy patriotism evaporated, and they seated themselves on the grass, to watch the approaching raft.

It had been a long and difficult passage, but at last the Bunkers landed.

"Hollo, Tony," said Tim, as he leaped ashore; "what are you doing here?"

"Been firing crackers," replied Tony.

"Got any more?"

"I haven't."

"Who has?"

"None of us," replied Frank. "We have **fired** them all."

"You lie! you haven't!" answered Tim, with an oath.

"I tell you the truth; don't I, Charley?"

"We had but six bunches, and we have used them all," added Charles.

"I don't believe it; you long-face fellers will lie twice as quick as one of us," said Tim, walking up to Frank.

"I have no more; I would not lie about it," protested Frank.

" Yes, yer would lie about it, too. Now, just hand over some o' them crackers, or I'll duck you in the lake."

Frank made no reply to this rude speech. He heartily wished himself off the island, and out of the company of the new comers.

' Hit him, Tim ! " cried one of the Bunkers.

" Hit him ! " repeated the others.

" Want to fight ? " said Tim, doubling up his fists, and assuming a pugilistic attitude.

" No, I don't want to fight; I will not fight," replied Frank, retreating backwards from the quarrelsome boy.

" O, you won't fight, eh ? Then you'll git licked," replied Tim, following him.

" I have not injured you ; I don't see why you should wish to fight with me."

" You lie ! yer have. Didn't yer tell me yer hadn't got no more crackers ? "

" I have not."

" Yes, yer have ; " and Tim struck Frank a severe blow, which made his lip bleed.

"Don't do that again!" cried Tony Weston, his face flushed with indignation.

"What are you going to do about it?" said Tim, turning to Tony.

"I don't want to fight; but I won't see him abused in that shape."

"Never mind him, Tony," interposed Frank. "He didn't hurt me much. Let us go over to the other side of the island."

"No, yer won't!" said Tim Bunker, approaching Frank again, and giving him another blow in the face.

Tony Weston could bear no more, and springing upon the leader of the Bunkers, he struck him several times in rapid succession.

"Don't, Tony, don't," said Frank, trying to separate the combatants.

"Fair play!" cried the Bunkers.

Tony, though younger and lighter than his antagonist, pressed him so severely that he brought him to the ground, before Frank and Charles could draw him off. Tim instantly leaped to his feet again.

"Come on!" said he.

" Don't, Tony."

" Mind your own business ! " said Tim to Frank, as he renewed the assault upon him.

Frank tried to get away, and when Tony and Charles came to his assistance the other Bunkers attacked them, and the fight became general.

" Give it to 'em," shouted Tim, as he struck his opponent several times on the head.

Frank saw that he had nothing to hope for unless he defended himself. He had done his best to prevent the fight, and now he felt justified in resorting to necessary violence, to save himself from further injury.

Suddenly springing upon his assailant, he bore him to the ground, and held him there. In the mean time, Tony and Charles were getting the worst of it, when a loud shout arrested the attention of the combatants. They all suspended the strife.

" It is Uncle Ben," said Charles.

The Bunkers seemed to understand the character of the old sailor, and taking to their heels, they fled precipitately towards the other end of the island.

"What are you about, boys?" said Uncle Ben, sternly, as he landed.

"We could not help it, Uncle Ben; indeed we could not," replied Frank, wiping his bleeding lip, and proceeding to tell the particulars of the whole affair.

"It was my fault; I ought not to have left you here alone. What will your father say?" said Uncle Ben, looking much troubled.

"He will not say any thing; I am sure you are not to blame, Uncle Ben."

"Jump into the boat, and let us be off. These boys must be attended to."

Uncle Ben, instead of immediately following the boys into the boat, pushed off the raft from the shore, and attaching a line to it, made fast the other end to the boat.

"What are you going to do, Uncle Ben?" asked Frank.

"I am going to keep them prisoners for a while," replied he, as the boat shot away from the island with the raft in tow.

"You don't mean to keep them there?"

" I sartinly do, till your father comes home, and
he may do what he pleases with 'em. If I had my
way, I'd tie 'em up to the grating and give 'em a
dozen apiece. 'Twould sarve 'em right, the meddle-
some rascals! I like good boys; but such boys as
them is worse nor marines."

" But, Uncle Ben, we can't sail with this raft
dragging after us."

" We will make the shore with it then."

The raft was towed ashore, and the boys had a
fine sail the entire length of the lake. As they
passed Centre Isle, they could see the Bunkers gathered in a ring, apparently discussing their prospects;
and on their return, Tim hailed them, begging to be
taken ashore.

" What do you say, boys? shall we forgive 'em? "
asked Uncle Ben.

" Yes! " exclaimed all three.

Uncle Ben landed at the island and took them in,
and during the passage read them a severe lecture
on the error of their ways. They gave good attention to him, and seemed very penitent. But no
sooner had they got ashore, and out of reach of the

old sailor, than they insulted him by hooting his name, coupled with the most opprobrious epithets.

"No use to be easy with 'em. The better you use 'em the worse they sarve you," said Uncle Ben, as he hauled the boat into its house.

6

CHAPTER V.

THE CLUB BOAT.

For a fortnight the Bunkers did not venture to approach the residence of Captain Sedley. The raft, which Uncle Ben had been instructed to break up, was removed some distance down the lake before he had time to execute his orders. After a few days, the memorable incident of the " fourth " ceased to be talked about, and was finally forgotten.

Two weeks passed away. Uncle Ben had been absent from home three days. He went to Boston with his employer, who returned without him. To Frank's earnest inquiries as to where he was, his father only replied that he would return soon.

It was after nine o'clock in the evening on the third day when he returned. Frank teased him to tell where he had been all the time ; but Uncle Ben only looked strange and mysterious, and would not gratify his curiosity.

Frank got up the next morning quite early, and walked over to the widow Weston's with Charles. On their return, a new object on the lake attracted the attention of the latter.

"Hollo, Frank! what's that?" exclaimed he. "By gracious! it is a new boat."

. "So it is; and what an odd-looking craft!"

Both boys ran with all their might down to the little beach by the road to get a nearer view of the strange boat.

"My eyes! look at it!" ejaculated the wondering Charles.

"What can it mean? It wasn't there last night," said Frank.

"No; and it looks like the boats we read about in the fairy books. I shouldn't wonder if it dropped down out of the clouds. Isn't she a beauty?"

"That she is! And how long and slender she is!"

"One, two, three — twelve places for the oars," cried Charles.

"Uncle Ben knows something about her, I know!" exclaimed Frank, as a beam of intelligence penetrated his mind.

"Just twig the bow! 'Tis as sharp as a razor."

"And there is her name on each side of it —
'Zephyr'! What a pretty name it is!"

"So it is. That boat's a ripper, let me tell you!"
said Charles, enthusiastically.

"A what?" asked Captain Sedley, coming down
from a thicket in the grove close by, where he had
been enjoying the astonishment of the boys.

"O father!" exclaimed Frank, "whose is she?
Where did she come from? What is it for?"

"One question at a time, Frank. But before I
answer any of them, let me say a word to you
Charles. You said she was a 'ripper' just now."

"That wasn't any harm, was it?"

"Not a very elegant word though. I will warrant
you cannot find it in the dictionary."

"I merely meant that it was a very fine boat."

' I presume you meant nothing wrong; but such
expressions do not add any thing to the force of language; and using them may induce a bad habit. If
you associated with boys accustomed to use profanity, this desire to use strong words would lead you
into the practice."

" I never thought of that."

" Just now you said, ' By gracious ! ' Such phrases are apt to induce profanity, and are no addition whatever to the force of your remark."

" I don't know as they are."

" You were very much surprised at seeing this boat."

" We were, indeed."

" Frank, it is yours," added Captain Sedley, turning with a smile to his son.

" Mine, father ! " exclaimed Frank, clapping his hands.

" It is yours, and of course your friends will derive as much pleasure from its use as you will yourself."

" But where did it come from, father ? "

" Two months ago, when the Bunkers first began to amuse themselves with the raft, the idea of procuring it occurred to me. I saw that you and Charles both had a great desire to join in their sport. For obvious reasons, I could not permit Frank to do so ; but I immediately resolved that you should have the means of enjoying yourselves in safety and comfort, and I ordered this boat to be built."

" Isn't she a beauty ! " exclaimed Charles.

" But, Charles, do you remember what you said a fortnight ago ? "

" No, sir."

" When you were talking here on the evening before the fourth of July ? "

" I said a great many things, I suppose, and some of them not quite so bright as they might have been," replied Charles, wondering what weakness of his was now to be exposed.

" Your remark was to the effect that boys who were obliged to mind their parents were the losers for their obedience."

" But I did not mean so, sir."

" You meant some of it, Charles. You wanted to go on the raft, and you felt at that moment as though it was a severe task to obey your parents. But I think it was only a momentary feeling."

" I am sure it was, sir."

" Let this beautiful boat, then, convince you that

obedience to your parents is your duty, as it ought
to be your pleasure."

"How came it here, father?" asked Frank. "I
am completely mystified."

"Uncle Ben has been in Boston the past three
days, procuring its outfit; and yesterday it was
brought up to the village on the railroad."

"That's why you would not tell me where he
was."

"It is; I thought I would surprise you. Last
night after dark Uncle Ben and I rowed it up from
the village."

"Wasn't we surprised, though?" added Frank.

"I'll bet we were," replied Charles.

"What, Charles, more of your inelegant speeches?" said Captain Sedley.

Charles blushed.

"I didn't mean to; I will try and break myself
of that habit."

"Do; it is a foolish practice."

"But, father, what shall we do with her? Has
the got any sails?" asked Frank.

"No, my son. It is what is called a club boat.

It is pulled with twelve oars. In Boston and a great many other places, a number of young men form themselves into a little society for the purpose of amusing themselves with these boats. You perceive it is built very long, narrow, and sharp, so as to attain the greatest speed; and rowing it is a very pretty exercise, as well as the most exciting amusement."

"I should think it would be; but, father, can't we get into it, so as to see what it is like?"

"Not now. To-day is Wednesday, and this afternoon Uncle Ben shall give you your first lesson in rowing."

"Can we row it alone?" asked Frank, looking perplexed as he saw the twelve rowlocks.

"No, Frank, you must form a society, a club, as they do in the city. You must have thirteen boys; twelve to row and one to steer."

"Hurrah! won't that be fine!" exclaimed Charles, with enthusiasm.

"But, boys, you must be careful whom you invite to join the club. We do not want any bad boys — especially none of the Bunkers."

" Not one of them," added Charles, promptly.

" Tony shall be one," said Frank.

" Tony is a good boy," replied Captain Sedley.

" Fred and Sam Harper," suggested Charles.

" They are very well ; but I shall leave the selection of the club to you, boys," continued Captain Sedley. " I am going to have a boat house built by the side of the other for your boat, and in one end of it will be a room for your meetings."

" That will be slick !" ejaculated Charles. " Won't we have the fun ! "

" You must make a kind of constitution; that is, some regulations for the government of the club."

" You will make those for us, won't you, father ? " said Frank.

" No ; I prefer that you should make them yourselves."

" We don't know how."

" I can tell you something about it. In the first place, you will want a clerk and a coxswain."

" A what ? " asked both boys together.

" A coxswain. When you sail he steers the boat,

and has the command; and when you hold a meeting he will be the chairman."

"Who will be coxswain?" said Charles, with a look of interest at Frank.

"You will choose him by vote, as well as the clerk."   .

"But the regulations, father."

"You must have no profanity, no lying, no vulgar language; and no boy must be permitted to neglect his school, or his duties at home, on account of the boat."

"We can fix all that," said Charles.

"I intend that this club shall be a society for the promotion of your moral welfare, as well as a means of amusement. In your club room I am going to place a library for your use, and next winter, when the lake is frozen over, you can meet there for amusement and instruction."

"That will be first rate," added Charles.

"What time shall we meet this afternoon, father?"

"Two o'clock, say. Now go to your breakfasts, and get ready for school. Be careful and not let the pleasure you anticipate interfere with your studies," said Captain Sedley, as the boys bounded away to their respective homes.

Frank and Charles, on their way to school, decided upon the boys whom they should invite to join the club, and in the course of the forenoon they were asked to assemble on the beach, without being told the precise object of the meeting.

The boys' heads were so full of the club boat that it required a great deal of courage to enable them to study in school that day ; but so closely had Captain Sedley connected the idea of improvement with the club, that they struggled hard, and succeeded in getting "perfect lessons."

CHAPTER VI.

THE EMBARKATION.

At half past one the members of the embryo boat club were on the beach. Those who were not informed before their arrival of the nature of the "time" in store for them, were in ecstasies when they beheld the beautiful boat reposing so lightly and gracefully on the tranquil bosom of the clear lake. None of them had ever seen such a fairy bark before, and it more than realized their most enthusiastic idea of the airy and graceful skiffs of which they had read and thought.

Uncle Ben had not arrived yet; but he had evidently been there during the forenoon, for the boat had been loosed from her moorings, and was now secured by a line attached to a stake driven in the sand.

The boys, as a matter of course, were very impatient to take their first lesson in rowing, and to skim over the glassy lake in the splendid barge before them.

"Where is uncle Ben?" asked Charles, hardly able to control his impatience.

"He will be here soon; it is not two o'clock yet," answered Frank.

"Don't be in a hurry, Charley," added Tony, who had seated himself upon the sand, and considering the exciting circumstances of the day, demeaned himself like a philosopher.

"I am so anxious to get a peep at the inside of her," replied Charles, as he took hold of the line that held the boat, and pulled her towards the shore. "Don't you think he will be here before two o'clock?"

"I don't know; I wouldn't touch her, Charley," said Frank.

"See how she shoots ahead! I scarcely pulled at all on the line."

The light bark, under the impulse of Charles's gentle pull, darted up to the shore, throwing her sharp bow entirely out of the water.

"Don't, Charley; you will scrape her keel on the

7

sand," interposed Frank. "She is built very lightly, and my father says she cost him four hundred
dollars."

"I won't hurt her. Just twig the cushioned seats
in the stern, and see all the brass work round the
sides! My eyes, how it shines!" exclaimed Charles,
holding up both hands with delight.

"Just see the oars," added Fred Harper.

"And there are the flags rolled up in the stern,"
said another boy.

"Won't we have a glorious time!" continued
Charles, as he placed one foot in the bow of the
boat.

"Don't get in, Charley; that isn't fair," interposed Tony Weston.

"It won't do any harm;" and Charles stepped
into the boat.

Half a dozen other boys, carried away by the ex
citement of the moment, followed his example, and
jumped in after him. Charles led the way to the
stern of the boat, walking over the seats, or, to speak
technically, the "thwarts."

The light boat, which had been drawn far out of

the water, and which now rested her keel upon the bottom, having no support upon the sides, rolled over on her gunnel, and tumbled the boys into the lake.

" There! Now see what you have done!" cried Tony, springing up, and pushing the boat away from the shore.

" Avast, there! What are you about?" exclaimed Uncle Ben, hobbling down to the beach as fast as his legs would carry him.

" You are too bad, Charley!" said Frank. "You will spoil all our fun by your impatience."

" I didn't think she would upset so easy," replied Charles.

" You ought not to have meddled with her."

" That you hadn't, youngster," said Uncle Ben. " Don't you know a boat can't stand alone when the keel is on the sand?"

The old sailor spoke pretty sternly, and Charles was abashed by his reproof.

" Forgive me, Uncle Ben; I didn't mean any harm."

" I know you didn't, Charley; but you must be

careful always. Live and larn," replied Uncle Ben, mollified by the penitence of the boy.

" She won't tip over again, will she ? " asked Frank.

" Not if you handle her right ; run over to that rock in the grove, where the water is deep, and I will bring her over."

Uncle Ben unfastened the line, and wading out a little way into the lake, jumped in, and rowed over to the rock.

" Now, my lads, you must do every thing in order. We don't want any hurrying and tumbling about. When you get into the boat, step easy, and keep quiet in your places," said Uncle Ben, as he brought the boat alongside the rock. " Fend off, there ! Don't let her rub ! "

Tony, who was by far the coolest and most reliable boy of the party, took hold of the boat, and prevented her from striking the rock.

" Now, Tony, you shall be stroke oarsman ; that is, you shall pull the foremost oar. You may get in first, and take that boathook forward. Stop, no more of you yet ; keep perfectly cool ! "

Tony obeyed, and took his station in the bow, with the boathook in his hand.

"Now hook on the rock with it, and keep her steady. There, that will do," continued Uncle Ben, taking another boathook and steadying the stern. Now, one at a time, and each of you take one of the seats."

The boys were so impatient that they could not wait to get in as the old sailor directed, and all huddled in together, to the imminent peril of their lives and the boat.

"Avast! that won't do! Back, all of you!" roared Uncle Ben, provoked by their awkwardness. "Now, Frank, call them by name, one at a time, and let each get his place before you call another."

This plan worked better. Uncle Ben was a firm advocate of discipline, and insisted on having every thing done in "shipshape order," as he styled it. The boys were all seated, and finding that their hurry and impatience only retarded their progress, they learned to keep still and wait till the old sailor old them what to do.

They had all seated themselves on one side of the

7 *

boat, and the consequence was, it nearly tipped her over.

"Now, my lads, trim ship. You are all over on the starboard side," said Uncle Ben, as he pushed the boat away from the rock.

The boys, in their eagerness to render a prompt obedience, all passed over to the opposite ends of the thwarts, and the boat instantly careened upon the other side.

"Avast there! Now stop a bit," continued the old sailor. "I am going to number you all. I don't know your names, all of you; so just mind the figgers. Tony, you are number one; say it."

"One," shouted Tony, with a pleasant laugh.

"The boy on the next seat."

"Two."

"Stop a bit; we have got one too many. One of you must ·be coxswain. Cap'n Sedley says you must choose him by vote. Who shall be your cox-swain, boys?"

"Frank Sedley," shouted all the boys together.

'Good! it is a unanimous vote," said Uncle Ben.

"You desarve the honor, Frank ; take a seat in the starn. Next boy, number."

"Three."

"Next."

"Four."

The boys all numbered, with the exception of Frank Sedley, who was not to pull an oar.

"Now, my lads, remember your numbers — don't touch the oars yet. You have got a good deal to larn fust," continued Uncle Ben.

"We shall be good scholars," said Charles.

"I hope you will. Now, Tony, take your place on the starboard side, opposite the rowlock over to port."

Tony, at a venture, seated himself on the forward thwart.

"Avast! that's the larboard side."

"But, Uncle Ben, we don't know the meaning of those words," added Frank.

"No more you don't," answered Uncle Ben, hitching up his trousers, and laughing good naturedly. "You can larn, though, if you pay 'tention."

"We will try."

"This side, then;" and the old sailor laid his hand upon the right hand side of the boat,—"this is the starboard side."

"The right hand side is the starboard side," repeated several of the boys.

"Number five," said Uncle Ben, calling upon Charles Hardy, "which is the starboard side?"

"This," replied Charles, pointing to *his* right.

"No, 'tain't."

"But you said the right hand side."

"No, I didn't; I said *this* side," replied the old sailor, laughing at the boy's perplexity. "It is the right hand side lookin' for'ad. Do you understand it now?"

"We do," shouted the boys together.

"Now, who can tell me which is the larboard side?"

"The left, looking forward," replied several.

"Good, my hearties; and larboard and port mean the same thing."

"We all understand it," said Charles Hardy.

"You'll forget it, ten to one, before to-morrow."

"No, we won't."

"Now, Tony, the starboard side. That's it. Number two, take the port side. That's right, Number three, the starboard."

The boys had grown more tractable, and Uncle Ben succeeded in getting them all in their proper places. The boat thus trimmed sat even on the water, and the boys were delighted with this change in her position. Most of them were wholly unaccustomed to boats, and the one-sided posture gave them a sensation of uneasiness. But while they saw Uncle Ben and some of the others feeling so secure, they did not like to acknowledge their timidity.

"When you take the oars, — not yet — don't be in a hurry. Do every thing calmly," said Uncle Ben. "You'll never larn any thing, if you don't go to work shipshape."

"But what shall I do?" asked Frank. "There are only twelve oars."

"Seat yourself square in the starn."

Frank obeyed, and Uncle Ben shipped the rudder. Instead of a tiller there was a short piece of wood, elegantly carved and gilded, which extended crossways with the boat. At each end of it was fastened a line, by means of which the rudder was moved.

"Take the lines, Frank, and keep quiet till we get ready to pull," said Uncle Ben, as he seated himself by the side of the young coxswain.

"We are all ready," interposed Charles Hardy, by way of hurrying the old sailor's movements.

"Now, take the oars."

All was confusion in an instant, and the boys began to "scrabble" with all their might. They handled their oars so awkwardly that many of them got rapped on the head, and one had his straw hat knocked overboard.

"That won't do, my lads," said Uncle Ben, as he drew in the lost hat with the boathook. "That was awful clumsy. Put 'em all back again."

The boys reluctantly obeyed. Uncle Ben declared it was "no sort of use" to try to do any thing, if they couldn't keep cool. He pointed out to them how the oars should be laid in the boat when they were "unshipped," and gave the order again.

"When I say 'Up,' take your oars and stand 'em on end. Now put 'em down again."

The oars were again deposited in their places.

" Up ! "

Up went the oars.

"Very well; but number two has it wrong. Put the blade of the oar up."

Number two changed the position of his oar.

"Hold 'em up parfectly straight," continued the instructor, as he glanced at the rows of oars. "Now, down again, all together."

The oars dropped with admirable precision, and Uncle Ben was perfectly satisfied with this manœuvre.

"Up!" cried he again, and up came the oars, man-of-war style. "Right! Now, when I say 'Down,' drop 'em into the rowlocks; but don't be clumsy about it. Down!"

Down came the oars into the water, all together, it is true, but Charles Hardy lost his overboard by his awkwardness.

CHAPTER VII.

PULL AWAY.

THE oar was regained, and Charles admonished to be more careful. Captain Sedley had witnessed the latter part of the drill from the shore, and the blunders of the boys, as well as their earnestness, afforded him a great deal of amusement.

Uncle Ben practised the two exercises he had explained, until his crew were as perfect as could be expected after one lesson.

"That was very well done, Ben," said Captain Sedley, when the boys had completed one of the exercises.

"Ay, ay, sir; that will do."

"Let us row now, Uncle Ben?" asked Charles.

"Pretty soon, my boy; don't be impatient. The third movement is to get the oar ready to drop into the water before the stroke. Now, throw the handles of the oars aft, and bend your bodies in the same direction."

The boys obeyed, and the instructor regulated the posture of each by his number, till the oars were all at the same height from the water.

" That will do ; now drop them into the water, and pull one stroke."

The movement was executed, but several of the boys, in their eagerness to pull a " strong stroke," did not dip deep enough, and were tumbled over backwards.

Captain Sedley laughed heartily.

" Rowing dry," said Uncle Ben, joining in the laugh. " Now, boys, when you pull, dip your oar so as to cover the blade. Try again. Ready ! "

The boys took the required position.

" Pull ! "

This time it was executed much better, but with a great deal of splashing and confusion, and the boat darted ahead under the impetus thus given.

" Hurrah ! " said Charles Hardy. " Here we go."

" Ready again," said Uncle Ben. " Pull ! "

The crew gained rapidly in skill, and after a great

8

many trials, they were able to pull the stroke all together.

"Frank, you must give the word, Unship your oars, and be ready."

The oars were all deposited in their proper places without the least confusion, and with admirable precision.

"Now, Frank, give the word."

"Up," said Frank, who could not refrain from laughing at his novel position.

All the oars came up as one.

"Down," said Frank.

The oars fell into the rowlocks.

"Good!" ejaculated Uncle Ben.

"Ready," continued Frank.

The boys took the required position.

"Pull."

"Bravo!" exclaimed Uncle Ben. "That was very well done."

"But can't we pull more than one stroke?" asked Charles.

"One at a time. Now, boys, the coxswain regulates the stroke of the oars by the motion of his

body.   When he wants you to pull, he bends forward, in this manner ; " and the old sailor swayed
his shoulders forward as he spoke.   "You must keep
your eye on him, and pull as he moves.   Try them
again, Frank."

"Ready," said the coxswain.   "Pull."

"Now bend forward, Frank, slowly and regular,
like the pend'lum of a clock."

Frank followed this direction, and the rowers took
half a dozen strokes with tolerable regularity.

"Mind your helm ; starboard a little — the other
way — that will do."

The boat was propelled with considerable speed
through the water, and the boys were in ecstasies at
their success.   Frank swayed his body to and fro,
with a slow and measured movement, and considering the trifling practice they had had, the rowers
worked with a tolerably good degree of regularity.
The stroke did not suit Uncle Ben, but he permitted
them to pull half way across the lake before he
stopped them to give further instructions.

When they reached the middle of the lake, he took
Frank's place at the helm, and drilled them for near-

ly an hour. They proved to be such apt pupils, that when the coxswain resumed his place, they could pull a regular man-of-war stroke with ease and precision.

" Now, my boys, you can pull up the lake ; but it will take a great deal of practice to make you perfect."

" Let us go down to Rippleton Village," suggested Charles Hardy.

" Rippleton it is ! " shouted several.

" Won't their eyes stick out down there ! "

" Better wait till you can row better than you do now, before you show yourselves much," added Uncle Ben.

" Up the lake then," said Frank.   " Pull."

Uncle Ben's drill in the middle of the lake enabled them sensibly to increase their speed, and before they were aware, they had reached the shore a mile and a half from Captain Sedley's house.

" Now, boys, you may go ashore and rest yourselves."

" We don't want to rest ; we are not tired," exclaimed several.

" We won't row any more, just yet."

" Uncle Ben, where are the flags? We haven't put them up yet."

" Here they are. The blue silk one, with silver stars around the letter ' Z,' goes in the bow. Put it in its place, Tony.

" And this American flag goes in the stern. Put it up, Frank," continued Uncle Ben.

The gay colors were raised, and the boys could scarcely contain themselves, so great was their delight at this new addition to their craft. It made her look so janty and gay, and seemed to give the finishing glory to the beautiful bark.

" Now, my lads, three cheers for the American flag. One!"

" Hurrah!"

" Two."

" Hurrah!"

" Three."

" Hurrah!"

" And long may it wave!" added Uncle Ben, heartily. " Boys, can't you sing?"

" 'Ve sing in school," replied several.

8 *

"Sing me a song, then, while we rest."

"What shall we sing?"

"Any thing you please."

"Canadian Boat Song," suggested Frank.

"Ay, ay, give us that."

Fred Harper was a good singer, and started the song. The boys all joined in, and Uncle Ben was so pleased when they had finished it, that he begged them to sing it again. They cheerfully complied, and the old man listened to the repetition with the most intense delight.

"Now, boys, I will sing you a sea song, if you like."

"Hurrah! do, Uncle Ben," exclaimed Charles.

Uncle Ben's voice was somewhat cracked and harsh, but he rendered with tolerable effect the song, —

> " 'Twas in the good ship Rover,
>   I sailed the world around;
> For twenty years and over,
>   I ne'er touched British ground."

"Bravo, Uncle Ben. Fred Harper, can't you give

us Ben Bolt and Sweet Alice?   I am sure Uncle Ben will like it."

" I will try," replied Fred.

" We will join the chorus."

The song was sung, and the old sailor shed a tear over " Sweet Alice, so young and so fair."

" Here comes father in the sailboat," cried Frank, as he discovered Captain Sedley approaching in his pleasure yacht.

" Ay, beating up agin the wind."

" Can't we have a race with him?" asked Charles Hardy.

" Sartin, if you like.   There is a fresh breeze springing up."

" The boys waited patiently until Captain Sedley reached the spot.

" How do you like your craft, boys?" asked he, as he threw his boat up into the wind, alongside the Zephyr.

" First rate!" they exclaimed with one voice.

" Three cheers for Captain Sedley," cried Tony Weston, taking off his cap and swinging it round above his head.   "One!"

" Hurrah ! "

" Two ? "

" Hurrah ! "

" Three ! "

" Hurrah ! " and the boys all clapped their hands for several moments.

Captain Sedley took off his hat, and politely returned his acknowledgments. When boys get to cheering, they hardly know when to stop; and when Fred Harper proposed three for Uncle Ben, there was a prompt and hearty response to the call.

" I'm much obleeged to you, boys, for the compliment," said the veteran, pulling off his tarpaulin.

" Now for the race," cried Charles.

Uncle Ben explained the wishes of the boys to Captain Sedley, and he readily agreed to a trial of speed, with the remark that he should expect to be beaten.

" Let me get my boat under good headway before you start," continued he, as he hauled aft his gib sheet and brought the boat before the wind.

The boat's crew waited till he had got nearly the eighth of a mile from them.

" Don't get excited, boys ; the wind is freshening," said Uncle Ben. " Now, Frank."

Frank gave the word which brought the oars to their perpendicular position, then to drop them into the water, and finally to pull.

" Steady, now," added Uncle Ben.

The Zephyr darted like an arrow through the water under the impetus of the twelve oars. Frank, in his anxiety to win the race, began to sway to and fro so rapidly, that Uncle Ben was obliged to caution him several times to keep cool.

" We are overhauling him very rapidly," said he ; " if you pull regular and save your strength, you will pass him before you get half way to the beach. Steady, Frank ; don't hurry them."

The boys pulled steadily, and as the old sailor had predicted, they passed Captain Sedley's boat long before they came to the beach. As the Zephyr shot passed him, a long, loud cheer burst from her crew.

" Isn't this fun ! " exclaimed Charles Hardy.

" Glorious ! " replied Joseph Barton, who was at he next oar before him.

" What do you think the Bunkers would say if they should see us about this time ? "

" Wouldn't they stare ! "

" Rest ! " said Frank ; and the boys ceased rowing, while the boat continued to shoot through the water with scarcely diminished velocity.

" There are the Bunkers on their raft," said Tony Weston, pointing down the lake.

All eyes were turned in the direction indicated by the speaker.

" You can pull down by them, if you like," added Uncle Ben.

" Pull ! " said Frank.

The Zephyr darted down the lake, and in a few moments was within hail of the raft.

" Not a word to them," said Uncle Ben.

" Can't we cheer them once ? " asked Charles.

" Yes, if you can keep good natur'd about it."

" We can."

The club boat shot by the raft, on which the wondering Bunkers stood like so many statues.

" Rest ! " said Frank.   " Now for three cheers."

They were given ; but the Bunkers were too much

bewildered by the appearance of the gorgeous boat, with its silken flags and bright colors, its gilded sides, and its graceful shape, to heed the cheers of the club.

" Pull! " said Frank; and under the direction of Uncle Ben, he managed the helm so as to make the Zephyr describe a graceful semicircle round the raft.

" Five o'clock," said the old sailor ; " we must go ashore."

Frank steered for the rock where they had embarked, Tony " fended off " with the boathook when they reached it, and the club separated for the night, leaving the boat in charge of Uncle Ben.

CHAPTER VIII.

THE STOLEN WALLET.

At school the next day, the club boat was the principal topic of conversation among the boys. Those who had been invited to join the club were regarded as especially fortunate. Frank Sedley was a distinguished personage, and even Tim Bunker unbent himself in some measure from his ferocious dignity in his attempts to conciliate him.

"I say, Frank, you will give me a sail in your boat, won't you?" said Tim.

"I should be very glad to accommodate you, but I don't think my father will let me take any boys who do not belong to the club."

"Can't I join the club?"

"It is full now."

"You can just make room for one more if you have a mind to."

"There are only twelve oars."

The school bell rang then, and Frank was glad to escape further importunity on the subject. Tim Bunker was dissatisfied with himself and every body else. He had seen the magnificent boat which Frank owned, and in which he and his companions had had such a glorious time on the preceding afternoon. He envied them the possession of the Zephyr, and he would have given any thing to have been permitted to join the club. Perhaps he would even have promised to become a better boy, for he keenly felt the weight of those moral obliquities which excluded him from the society of Frank and his friends.

But more especially did he envy Tony Weston his good luck in getting into the club; for Tony's admission was abundant evidence that the social standing of the boys had not been taken into consideration. There was no rich and poor about it; it was good and evil entirely. And Tim had always cherished a strong feeling of dislike, and even hatred, towards the poor widow's son, undoubtedly because he was a good boy, and every body liked him. He had not forgotten Tony's interference on the island, when he was about to thresh Frank Sedley, and among the

Bunkers he expressed his intention to be fully re-
venged.

At recess, Frank, Charles, and Tony went up to a
neighbor's house close by to get some water. When
they had drank, and were passing through the woodhouse to return, Charles observed an old wallet lying
on a bench.

"Twig!" said he, in his peculiar style.

"That must be Farmer Whipple's," replied Tony.

"Probably he laid it down when he was paying
somebody some money," added Frank.

"I will carry it to him," said Charles. "He is
out in the garden."

"Don't meddle with it," answered Tony. "We
will see him and tell him it is there."

"But somebody might steal it in the mean time."

"No they won't; I wouldn't meddle with it."

The boys walked off towards the school house,
but they did not find the farmer in the garden.

"He was here when we came up," said Tony.
"I will find him;" and he walked towards the
barn, while Charles and Frank continued on their
way.

Tony looked all about the premises, but he did not find the farmer. Returning to the wood house, he found that the wallet was gone.

" Hollo, Tony," said Tim Bunker, at this moment entering the wood house, and going to the well for a drink.

" Have you seen Farmer Whipple, Tim ? "

" Yes ; he just went into the house," replied the chief of the Bunkers.

" Which way did he go in ? "

" Right through this way. He was just ahead of you when you came from the barn."

" O, was he ? " said Tony, much relieved.

The farmer had taken his wallet then as he passed through, and he was satisfied it was all right.

" I say, Tony, what were you doing out to the barn ? Hooking eggs, eh ? "

" I was not," answered Tony, indignantly.

" Honor Bright ? "

" *I* am not a thief."

" I'll bet you ain't," drawled Tim, placing his thumb against his nose, and wagging his four fingers back and forth

Tony heard the school bell ring, and waiting foɪ no more, ran off with all his speed. Tim was so late that Mr. Hyde, the master, gave him a sharp reproof for loitering by the way.

Tim Bunker's seat was next to Tony's and though the former persisted in annoying him, whispering in his ear something about " sucking eggs," he tried to be patient and good natured. But, at last, when he could endure it no more, he informed against him.

" What do you mean by ' sucking eggs,' Tim ? " asked Mr. Hyde, after he had called him on the platform.

" I saw Tony skulking round Farmer Whipple's barn at recess."

" Did you see him have an egg ? "

" No, sir ; but I thought he had been eating something."

Mr. Hyde investigated the case fully, and Tim got punished for his conduct in annoying his schoolmate.

School was dismissed as usual, and the boys went home. In the afternoon, Tony had some work to do, and did not come.

A few minutes after two, when the boys were all

in, Farmer Whipple entered the room, apparently in a high state of excitement.

" Where is Tony Weston ? " said he.

" He is absent this afternoon," replied Mr. Hyde.

" I lost my pocket book this morning."

" Indeed ! "

" I saw Tony Weston and the Bunker boy in the wood shed a little before."

" It was Tim Bunker, then," added Mr. Hyde, in a low tone.

" I think's likely," continued Farmer Whipple ; " but Tony was there too."

" I will state the case, and see if the boys know any thing about it," said the master.

Mr. Hyde called the attention of the boys by ringing a little bell on his desk, and then mentioned the loss which Farmer Whipple had met with.

" If any scholar knows any thing about it, let him signify it."

Frank and Charles raised their hands.

" Frank ? "

" I saw a black wallet lying on the bench when we went up after some water."

9 *

" Who were with you ? "

" Tony and Charles."

" Any one else ? "

" No, sir."

" Why did you not take charge of it, and give it to Mr. Whipple ? "

" Tony thought we had better not touch it, and we decided to tell Mr. Whipple it was there as we went through the garden."

" But you didn't tell me," said the farmer.

" No, sir ; we didn't find you in the garden when we came back, and Tony went to look for you while we continued on our way."

" Has Tony said any thing to you about it since ? " asked Mr. Hyde.

" Yes, sir ; he told us after school that he didn't find Mr. Whipple, and when he went back to the wood house, the wallet was gone.   He met Tim Bunker there, who told him the owner had just gone in that way."

" Now I think on't, I paid a little bill, and I recollect of laying the wallet down on the wash bench," said Farmer Whipple.

" And Tim Bunker was there ? " asked the master.

" Not while we were," replied Charles.

" Tim ? "

" Sir," answered the chief of the Bunkers, promptly.

" Do you know any thing about this wallet ? "

" Don't know nothing about it."

" Were you up there ? "

" Yes, sir."

" You saw Tony there ? "

" Yes, sir ; when I was going up, I saw him come out of the barn and go into the wood house."

" Did you see Mr. Whipple ? "

" No, sir."

Frank and Charles looked at each other. Tim's story differed from Tony's.

" You saw Tony in the wood shed ? "

" When I went in, he was tucking away something in his pocket."

Tony's friends were utterly confounded by this bold statement.

" You didn't see what it was, did you ? " inquired Mr. Hyde, pained by the turn the affair was taking.

" I didn't. I thought it was an egg at first. He

was kind of struck up when I entered, and asked me if I had seen Farmer Whipple. I told him I hadn't. The bell rang then, and he cut away to school."

Tim's story seemed plausible; but the master could not harbor a suspicion that Tony was guilty of theft.

"Which pocket was it, Tim?" asked Farmer Whipple.

"The side pocket of his linen sack."

"Which side?"

"The left hand side."

"That will do," said Mr. Hyde; and he and Mr. Whipple conferred on the subject.

Frank was amazed. Tony steal the wallet! Impossible! He never could do such a thing.

The conference ended, and Farmer Whipple left the school room. Returning to his house, he harnessed his horse, and drove down to Squire Murdock's, the magistrate, to procure a warrant for the arrest of Tony. This he obtained, and after getting a constable to serve it, he drove to the widow Weston's.

Tony was in the garden picking some currants to

sell the following morning. He was hard at work, and his coat lay upon a bush near him.

Farmer Whipple and the constable jumped over the fence and approached him.

"How do you do, Mr. Whipple?" said Tony, suspending his occupation. "How do you do, Mr. Headley?"

"I am sorry to trouble you, Tony; but we've got some suspicions agin you," began Farmer Whipple.

"Against me!" exclaimed Tony, with a glance at the constable.

"Sorry for it, but it looks bad agin you."

"What have I done?" asked the poor boy, alarmed by the words of the farmer.

"I lost my wallet this morning, and Tim Bunker says he saw you tucking something into your pocket," replied Farmer Whipple, proceeding to detail all the circumstances.

"I am innocent!" pleaded Tony.

"But you were there?"

"I was there;" and Tony told his story, just as he had related it to Frank Sedley.

"All that may be, but you see, Tony, things are against you. Tim's story is as straight as can be. This is your coat, ain't it?"

"Yes; you can examine that, and search the house if you like."

The constable took the coat. The pockets were filled with various articles known in the vocabulary of a schoolboy. Mr. Headley thrust his hand in, and Tony confidently waited the result. Several things were taken out and returned. It was not in that pocket.

But the first thing the constable drew out of the other pocket was Farmer Whipple's wallet!

"No use, Tony," said Mr. Headley.

"I did not know it was there; I did not put it there!" protested the poor boy, whose face was as white as a sheet.

"You must come with me, Tony; I never would have believed it," said the constable.

The widow Weston was called and a statement of the case made to her. Poor, loving, devoted mother! her heart was wrung with agony. But there was a consolation for her. Tony could not be a thief! He was innocent, she was sure, however strong appearances might point to his guilt.

The constable took him into the wagon, and Farmer Whipple drove off to the Rippleton jail, which was located in the village.

CHAPTER IX.

TONY'S CASE.

No one of all Tony's numerous friends was more surprised at the accusation made against him than Captain Sedley. Like all who were familiar with the past life of the brave little fellow, he was incredulous. The very fact that Tim Bunker was near at the time of the alleged theft seemed to be sufficient to clear him. The finding of the wallet in his pocket was the most unaccountable piece of testimony that had been adduced against him. It did not seem probable that it would have remained so long in his pocket unknown to him, if any one had been so wicked as to place it there.

As soon as the wagon which bore Tony a prisoner to the Rippleton jail had gone, Mrs. Weston put on her bonnet, and hastened over to Captain Sedley's house. She was sure of finding assistance there. She was so confident of Tony's innocence, that the thought of proving it for the satisfaction of the public seemed superfluous.

"I am sure he never could do such a thing in the world, Captain Sedley," said she, wiping away her tears, and gazing with earnestness into the face of her benevolent patron.

"Tony always was honest," replied Captain Sedley.

"Honest! He would not steal the value of a pin from any body."

"I think he would not."

"I *know* he wouldn't!"

"But it seems very strange that the wallet should have been found in his pocket."

"Tim Bunker put it there, you may depend upon it."

"Very likely; but, Mrs. Weston, you know that all these things must be proved. As the affair stands now, I am afraid the testimony against him, notwithstanding his good character, will be quite sufficient to convict him."

"O Captain Sedley, I know he is innocent," exclaimed the poor widow, her eyes filling with tears again.

" But it must be proved, you see. The finding of the wallet upon him, and the testimony of Tim Bunker that he saw him putting something in his pocket, in the very place where the lost property was alleged to have been left, will leave scarcely a doubt in the minds of judge and jury."

" Tim Bunker did it, I know ! "

Captain Sedley shook his head. Though he had the fullest confidence in Tony's innocence, he desired to give his mother a perfect understanding of the difficulties of the case. After all, there was a remote possibility that poor Tony had been led to take the wallet, and if such should finally prove to be the fact, it was better for the widow to be prepared for the worst.

" I do not think Tony is guilty, Mrs. Weston; but you must consider that appearances are very strong against him," said he.

" I know it, sir. Poor Tony ! must he spend the night in jail ? Is there no way to get him out ? " sobbed the widow.

" He ,shall not want for a friend, Mrs. Weston. Farmer Whipple must have returned by this time, and I will go up and see him. But I do not think we can get him out to-day."

"Thank you, sir; you are very good. If I could only see him, and tell him that I feel sure he is innocent, the cold walls would seem less dreary to him. I know what the poor fellow is thinking about."

Mrs. Weston cried like a child when she thought of her darling boy, shut up within the narrow walls of a prison cell.

"He will be thinking of his home," continued she. "He will think of me."

"He has been a good son, Mrs. Weston."

"That he has, sir. Tony steal? No, sir. He thinks too much of his mother and his home to do such a thing. But don't you think I could see him?"

"I will see him myself; won't that do as well?"

"I don't know."

"I will tell him just how you feel about it — that you are confident he is innocent."

"Thank you, sir; he will be so comforted by it."

"And to-morrow he will probably be examined before the magistrate."

" Then he will discharge him, I know ! "

" I fear not ; if there are reasonable grounds for supposing him guilty, he will be committed to await the action of the grand jury."

" Then it will be weeks and months before they prove his innocence," interposed the widow.

" The grand jury is in session now ; all they will do, if they find a bill against him, will be to commit him for trial."

" That makes three times they will try him," said Mrs. Weston, perplexed by the complications of the law. " Must he stay in prison till all these trials are finished ? "

" He can be bailed out to-morrow, after his examination."

" I must give bonds for him, must I ? "

" I will do that, Mrs. Weston. Probably he can come home before to-morrow noon."

" God bless you, Captain Sedley. You have always been very good to me in my troubles."

" Ben," said Captain Sedley, going to the window, and calling the old sailor, who was at work in the garden — " Ben, put the bay horse into the chaise."

" 'This is a world of trouble, Captain Sedley," said the widow, with a deep sigh.

" But from trouble and affliction come forth our purest aspirations.   God is good to us even when he sends us trials and sorrows."

" I will not complain; I have much to be thankful for."

In a few moments, the horse and chaise were ready.

" I am going over to see Farmer Whipple, Mrs. Weston, and then I shall ride down to Rippleton. Keep your spirits up, and be assured every thing shall be done to comfort your son, and to prove his innocence.   I shall engage Squire Benson to defend him."

" Heaven bless you, Captain Sedley," said the poor widow, wiping away her tears, as her benevolent friend got into his chaise.

Farmer Whipple was fortunately at home when he arrived at his house, and Captain Sedley immediately opened his business.

" I don't much think that Tony did it," said the farmer; " but things were agin him, you see."

10 *

" How much money was there in the wallet? "
asked Captain Sedley.

" More'n I can afford to lose, cap'n. It was a
careless trick of mine."

" What was the amount? "

" There was forty-six dollars in bills, besides some
odd change."

" Do you remember what banks the bills were
on ? "

" Most on 'em. There was a twenty dollar bill on
the Rippleton Bank, a ten on the Village Bank, and
some small bills, mostly on Boston Banks."

" Where is the wallet now ? "

" I got it ; Squire Little said I might take it agin. '

" Was the money all right ? "

" Bless you, no ! If it had been, I wouldn't say
a word. All the small bills were there, but the big
ones were gone."

" Indeed ! "

" That's the wo'st on't."

" Have you any description of the lost bills ? "

" Well, yes ; I reckon I should know the twenty
agin, if I saw it."

" How ? "

" Well, it happens rather lucky. Arter we came from the jail, I went into Doolittle's store to git some tea. When I went in he was fixin' some kind of a plate, with his name on't ; a pencil plate, I believe he called it."

" A stencil plate," said Captain Sedley.

" Jest so ; he was marking his name on the back of some bank bills with it. I telled him about the robbery, and that the twenty dollar bill he give me the day before was gone with the rest. Then he telled me that that twenty dollar bill was marked with his ' pencil plate,' d'ye see ? "

" He might have marked a dozen others with it," added Captain Sedley.

" No, he didn't. You see he didn't git the plate till jest afore he paid me that bill, and he is sartin that is the only twenty dollar bill he has marked."

" Did you see the mark yourself ? "

" I saw sunthin on it, but I couldn't read it without puttin' my glasses on ; so I didn't mind what it was "

Captain Sedley considered this important information. If the twenty dollar bill, thus marked, should ever appear in the village, it might furnish a clew by which to trace out the thief.

On his arrival at Rippleton village, he went to Doolittle's store, and ascertained that he had marked no more bills ; that he was sure he had marked no other twenty dollar bill than the one he had paid to Farmer Whipple. Requesting him not to mark any more, he went over to the jail.

Tony was in much better spirits than he expected to find him. His only trouble was in relation to his mother, and he cried bitterly when he spoke of her. Captain Sedley comforted him, assuring him his mother and his friends were satisfied that he was innocent, and that he should have the best lawyer in the county to defend him.

" I don't want any lawyer, Captain Sedley," said Tony, stoutly; " I am as innocent of this crime as though I had never been born."

" But, Tony, who do you think stole the wallet?"

" I have no idea, unless Tim Bunker did, and has laid it to me to clear himself."

"Tim is one of the witnesses, and a good lawyer may be able to get the truth of him."

"I don't believe he could," replied Tony, with a faint smile.

"I shall engage Squire Benson to defend you, and to-morrow, before the examination, he will come in and see you. If you have any thing to say, you can say it to him."

"I can only say I am innocent."

"He will want to know all the circumstances."

"I will tell him all I know about it."

After some further conversation, Captain Sedley took his leave, and hastened to the office of Squire Benson, who was the most distinguished lawyer in that county.

The legal gentleman readily engaged to defend Tony, and arrangements were made for the examination. The marked bank bill was an important matter' for consideration, though there was no present hope of finding it. But there was a prospect that it would eventually come to light.

On his arrival at his house, Captain Sedley found the widow Weston waiting his return. She was much comforted when she heard that Tony was in good spirits. She listened with attention to all her kind friend said, and went home with a lighter heart than when she came. The interest which Captain Sedley manifested in the case inspired her with hope. He was an influential man, and his assistance would enable her to do all that could be done.

On the following morning, the examination of Tony took place at the office of Squire Little. Mrs. Weston had an interview with her son, when he was brought in by the officer. Both wept, but there was hope in the consciousness that he was innocent. Frank, Charles, and Tim Bunker were there as witnesses, as well as Farmer Whipple and Mr. Hyde.

The examination proceeded, but it was only a repetition of the facts we have already given. Squire Benson, in his cross examination, pressed Tim Bunker severely; but though there were several trifling inconsistencies in his answers, his testimony was generally accurate. He denied having told Tony that he saw Farmer Whipple pass through the woodhouse.

Captain Sedley had prepared Mrs. Weston for the

result, and when Tony was bound over to await the action of the grand jury, she heard the decision with tolerable calmness. Her benevolent friend became his bail; he was liberated, and they all went home together.

CHAPTER X.

THE BOAT HOUSE.

THE boat house for the Zephyr had been commenced on Wednesday, the day following her arrival. All the carpenters that could work upon it were engaged by Captain Sedley, so that by Saturday it was nearly finished.

Its location was at one end of the beach not far from the sailboat. It was fifty feet long, and extended out over the waters of the lake. It was built on piles, driven into the sand on the bottom. The club hall was at the land end of the building, and was about fifteen feet square. From this apartment the boys passed into the boat house proper, which was so arranged that they could all take their places in the boat, and push out into the lake without confusion or inconvenience.

But as my young friends undoubtedly feel a great desire to obtain an accurate idea of the situation and arrangements of the boat house, I have drawn a plan of it, which is here sub-joined.

If my young readers care-fully examine the plan, and refer to the explanations, they can understand the situation of every thing connected with the boat house.

Around the platform a railing was constructed with a gate at the bow, and one on each side of the boat, so that the mem-bers of the club could get into it only at these three places.

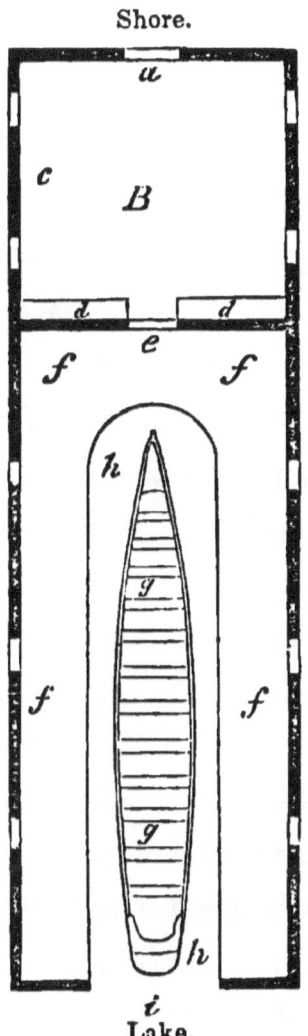

EXPLANATIONS. — *a*, the outside door; *B*, the club hall; *c*, stove; *d, d*, cases for the library; *e*, entrance to the boat hall; *f, f, f, f*, a platform; *g, g*, the boat; *h, h*, the water in which the boat floats; *i*, the door through which the boat passes out upon the lake.

Frank and Charles protested against this railing at first, and maintained that there was not the least danger of their falling into the water; but Captain Sedley, knowing how prone boys are to scuffle and be careless, insisted upon having it.

The boys watched the progress the carpenters made in erecting the boat house with the deepest interest, and Uncle Ben got almost out of patience answering the innumerable questions they put to him in regard to what every thing was for. Morning, noon, and night they visited the building, and longed for Saturday afternoon, when they were to make another excursion in the Zephyr.

Poor Tony's misfortunes had excited all their sympathy, and divided their attention with the club. Some of them ventured to doubt the innocence of their companion, though a large majority felt quite sure he would be cleared at the trial.

Early on Saturday afternoon, Frank and Charles met at the boat house.

" Will Tony come, do you think ? " asked the latter.

" I told him this morning to be sure and come. I hope he will."

" Do you think your father will let him continue to belong to the club ? " asked Charles.

" Certainly he will !   Why not ? "

" Only think of it — taken up for stealing ! "

" Do you believe he is guilty ? "

" They wouldn't put him in jail if he wasn't, it isn't likely."

" But he hasn't been tried yet."

" No ; but then to think that the wallet was found in his pocket."

" I don't believe he is guilty, any more than I believe I am," replied Frank, warmly.

" Nor I ; but —— "

" But what, Charley ? "

" Things look so against him."

" I am afraid Tim Bunker knows more about it than he chooses to tell."

" Don't you remember Tony didn't want us to meddle with it, and said we had better tell Farmer Whipple it was there, rather than touch it ourselves ? " added Charles, looking earnestly into the face of his companion.

" I *know* Tony wouldn't steal it."

" He might."

" I am surprised to hear you say so, Charley," said Frank, hurt by the doubts of his friend.

" He might have thought that Farmer Whipple would never have found him out."

" That wouldn't have made any difference with Tony."

" He might have thought, too, how much good the money would do his mother."

" Tony never could have thought that stolen money would do his mother any good."

" Perhaps he did not think any thing about the wickedness of the act."

" Is it possible, Charley, that you have so poor an opinion of Tony as that? I should not think you would wish to associate with him now."

" I don't know," said Charles, apparently absorbed by his own thoughts. " Do you think we ought to have him in the club till after this thing is settled? "

" Why, Charley! You can't think how it hurts my feelings to hear you talk so."

" What do you suppose your father will say about it ? "

"I know what he will say; he believes Tony is entirely innocent."

"O, if he does, *we* ought not to say a word," replied Charles, promptly. "Only, you know, he said so much about the club being a means of improvement as well as amusement."

Frank could not understand the thoughts of his friend; but his father, who had been instructing the workmen in regard to the boat house, joined them soon after, and the question was referred to him, with a statement of Charles's views.

Captain Sedley looked searchingly into Charles's eye.

"You think Tony ought to be excluded from the club, do you?" asked he.

"No, sir; *I* don't think so; but I didn't know but *you* might think so," replied Charles, confused by the earnestness of Captain Sedley's glance.

"Charles, I am afraid you have not made your mind up in regard to the question. You are willing to believe any thing that will please those whom you wish to conciliate."

"I want to believe the truth."

11*

" You are not so particular about the truth as you are about suiting your friends."

Captain Sedley had had a great deal of experience in reading the characters of men, and he readily perceived that Charles desired to be foremost in condemning evil, for the purpose of getting the good will of others. It was a dangerous state of mind, for with the Bunkers he would probably have been just as forward in a bad cause. His motive was not a worthy one. It was the same as that which sometimes induces men and women to go to church, to give money to the poor, or to assume a virtue they do not possess — for the reputation it would give them. It was the same motive which had urged him to give his money to the widow Weston.

Perhaps he was not fully conscious of his motive in thus being the foremost to condemn poor Tony; but Captain Sedley read his character rightly, and understood the workings of his mind.

" I am sure I feel kindly towards Tony ; as kindly as any other fellow in the club," said Charles.

" I do not doubt it ; but we must watch all our thoughts and actions."

Captain Sedley returned to the boat house to give further directions concerning the building. Before two o'clock, all the boys, with the exception of Tony Weston, were gathered on the beach.

"I hope he will come," said Frank, much concerned at the absence of his friend.

"I hope so," added Charles.

"Here is Uncle Ben. Hurrah!" shouted several of the boys.

"I arn't goin' with you this afternoon," said the veteran, as he laid an armful of oars, boathooks, and other furniture belonging to the Zephyr, which had been carried to the house for safe keeping, upon the beach.

"Not going with us, Uncle Ben?" asked Frank.

"Your father is going," replied the old sailor, as he drew the boat in shore, and put the oars and other articles on board.

"Here he comes," added Frank.

"Where is Tony?" asked Captain Sedley, as he discovered the absence of the widow's son.

"He has not come."

"I am sorry for that. We will go up and see

where he is. Ben, take the boat over to the flat rock."

" Ay, ay, sir."

The boys scampered over to the place of embarkation, followed by Captain Sedley.

" Frank, you may take Tony's place," said his father, when they reached the rock, "and I will steer."

Frank leaped into the bow of the boat, and took the boathook. Steadying her, he called the numbers, and the club all took their places in excellent order, and sat waiting for further commands.

" Very well, boys; your discipline is most excellent," said Captain Sedley. " Push off, Frank. Ready with the oars."

" Up!" said Uncle Ben, who stood on the rock.

The manœuvre was executed with admirable precision.

" Down ! "

The oars fell all together into the rowlocks.

" Ready ! " and the boys all bent forward, ready for the stroke.

" Pull ! " and away they flew.

Captain Sedley steered up the lake, in the direction of the widow Weston's cottage.

The Zephyr darted like an arrow through the water, her sharp bow cutting the tiny waves like a knife, making a most musical ripple as it dashed a clear jet of white foam as high as the gunwale.

It was scarcely three minutes before Captain Sedley ordered them to rest. The boat darted into a cove, by the widow's house, and Frank and his father landed.

Tony, it seemed, wished to join the club; but his mother, fearful lest some of the boys should taunt him with the occurrences of the past few days, desired him to remain at home. Captain Sedley's request, however, was quite sufficient, and Tony followed Frank down to the boat.

"Three cheers for Tony Weston!" exclaimed Charles Hardy, as they came in sight.

The cheers were given; but Captain Sedley could not but question the motives of him who had proposed them.

"Now, Frank, you are coxswain again," said Captain Sedley.

Tony took his place at the bow oar, and Frank in the stern sheets. The former was received with sympathy and kindness by the club, and the poor boy felt how pleasant it was to have the good will of his companions in the midst of his trials.

"Up!" said Frank, when all was ready for a start. "Down! Pull!" .

"Down the lake, Frank, towards the village," added Captain Sedley.

Again the beautiful Zephyr bounded over the waters; but after pulling a few minutes, Captain Sedley directed the club to cease rowing.

"Boys, we are going to have a uniform for the club," said he.

"A uniform!" repeated several of the boys.

"Hurrah!" shouted Charles Hardy.

"I have already spoken to Mr. Burlap, the tailor, and now I am going down to have him take your measures."

"What will the uniform be, father?" asked Frank.

"White sailors' trousers, a blue jacket, and a white shirt trimmed with blue. The hat will be a tarpaulin, with 'Zephyr,' in gilt letters, on the front."

The boys all clapped their hands, as the only means in their power to express their gratification.

" Now, pull for Rippleton."

. The Zephyr parted the waters before her graceful bow, and sped like a rocket on her way. The beautiful boat excited a great deal of attention at the village, and when the boys returned from the tailors, hundreds had collected on the bank to see them row.

Captain Sedley gratified the curiosity of the people by exercising the club for some time near the spot where they stood. After a row across the lake, they returned, and the Zephyr was moored in her new house, much to the delight of her enthusiastic crew.

CHAPTER XI.

THE FIRST MEETING IN ZEPHYR HALL.

In another fortnight the boat house was entirely completed, furnished, and ready for the occupancy of the club. School had closed for the season, and the summer vacation had commenced; but most of the boys, in anticipation of the pleasure which the boat club promised them, preferred to stay at home rather than visit their friends at a distance.

Mr. Burlap, the tailor, had exerted himself to the utmost, and the new dress of the boat club was ready for use. The tarpaulins had been purchased and lettered, and the uniforms had been hung up in the boat house. A nail was appropriated to each member, whose number was painted over it.

Uncle Ben had given the boys several lessons in rowing in the mean time, and the discipline of the club was pronounced perfect. The first meeting in the new hall was appointed to take place on Monday morning, and punctually to the hour, the members were all assembled.

The hall had been tastefully furnished and deco‑rated, under the direction of Captain Sedley. On the floor was a very pretty carpet with bright colors; on the walls hung several large engravings in frames, illustrative of various boat scenes; and over the door leading to the boat house proper was painted, in blue letters, —

ZEPHYR BOAT CLUB.

On the window curtains the name of the club was also painted. In the middle of the room was placed a long table, around which were arranged thirteen chairs for the members. The library cases were filled with books, which had been selected with great care by Mr. and Mrs. Sedley. On the table were placed various pamphlets and periodicals, and when the club assembled, Uncle Ben was there, seated in the coxswain's arm chair, poring over the pages of the Sailors' Magazine.

The boys all came in and took their chairs, each of which was numbered, and Uncle Ben cheerfully resigned his place to the coxswain.

"Order!" said Frank, rapping on the table.   .

Captain Sedley had instructed Frank in some of the forms of conducting a public meeting, and the matter had been made the topic of conversation among the others, so that they had a tolerable idea of parliamentary usage. They were all enthusiastic and eager to learn, and some of them had attended a special town meeting a few days before, for the purpose, as they expressed it, of "seeing how the thing was done." And when Captain Sedley came in to breakfast on the morning of the eventful day, he found Frank intently perusing the pages of Cushing's Manual.

When, therefore, the coxswain called the meeting to order, all noise and conversation immediately ceased, and they seemed determined to conduct themselves with better propriety than the "legal voters" of Rippleton had at the town meeting they had attended.

Frank, in the words of the newspaper reporters, "made a neat and appropriate speech," on the occasion of their taking possession of the new hall. After this important matter had been disposed of, the coxswain remarked that the first business of the club would be to select a name for the hall.

"Mr. Chairman," said Charles Hardy, rising with the utmost gravity and decorum.

Uncle Ben laughed outright; but immediately apologized for his unseemly mirth, and fearful lest he should disturb the dignified body again, he withdrew from the hall, and busied himself in polishing up the brass works of the boat.

"Charles Hardy," said the chairman, bowing to the member who had obtained the floor.

"I move that this hall, hereafter, henceforward, and for the time to come, be called Sedley Hall," said Charles, who, in the absence of any work on parliamentary tactics in his father's library, had carefully studied the Business Man's Assistant, from which he had stored his memory with a variety of legal and technical phrases. He had the jingle of them in his head, and did not mind much about the substance.

Captain Sedley entered the hall just as he made his motion.

"Second the motion," said Fred Harper.

"It is moved and seconded that our room be called Sedley Hall," continued the coxswain. "The question is open for discussion."

"Mr. Chairman," said Captain Sedley, scarcely able to control his inclination to indulge in a hearty laugh at the dignity and formality of the proceedings, "though not, strictly speaking, a member of the club, perhaps you will indulge me in a few remarks on the question before the house. I am deeply grateful to you for the honor to my name and family which is contemplated by the excellent member on the other side of the table, but for reasons of my own, I must beg the gentleman to withdraw his motion."

"He cannot withdraw without the consent of the house — of the club, I mean," said Frank, blushing at his blunder.

"It is customary when no objection is made," replied Captain Sedley, gravely, "to permit a motion to be withdrawn."

"Mr. Chairman," said Charles, rising, "for the obvious reasons mentioned by the honorable and distinguished gentleman, I withdraw my motion."

At the risk of disturbing the dignity of the meeting, Captain Sedley remarked that he had stated no reasons.

" I move that the room be called Zephyr Hall," said Tony Weston.

" Second the motion," said Charles.

Frank stated the question, and observed that it was open for any remarks. But the members, not feeling disposed to indulge in any flights of eloquence before Captain Sedley, maintained an obstinate silence for full five minutes. The chairman, impressed with the idea that some speeches must be made, any how, did not interrupt the dignified quiet by putting the question.

At last the silence was broken by a hearty laugh on the part of Captain Sedley.

" Why don't you put the question, Frank ? " asked he.

" The debate has not taken place yet."

" There are some questions which it is not necessary to debate."

" Question ! " said Fred Harper, who had been to town meeting.

12 *

" Those in favor of calling the room Zephyr Hall, please manifest it."

" All up ! " cried Fred Harper.

" It is a unanimous vote."

" Let the clerk record the vote," whispered Captain Sedley to his son.

" We have no clerk yet."

" Doing business without a clerk ! " laughed his father.

" The next business will be to choose a clerk," continued Frank, laughing. " Please to bring in your ballots for a clerk."

There were paper and pens at the other end of the table, and Fred Harper, who seemed to have a very good idea of " the manner in which the public business is transacted," commenced writing votes. In a few moments they were all supplied, and the ballots were deposited in the chairman's cap.

" Whole number of votes, thirteen," said Frank ; " necessary for a choice, seven ; Frederic Harper has one ; Anthony Weston has twelve, and is elected."

Captain Sedley clapped his hands at this evidence of good will on the part of the members, and the club all joined heartily in the demonstration. Three days before, the grand jury had found a bill against Tony, but his friends still continued to regard him as an innocent person.

" I thank you for your kindness," said Tony, rising ; " I am sure, I —— " but the poor fellow choked up, and could say no more.

His heart was full, and the great tears rolled down his cheeks.

" Never mind it, Tony ; here is the record book," said Fred Harper, taking it from the library case.

Tony wiped away his tears, and seated himself at the foot of the table, where a small desk had been placed for the use of the clerk.

" Mr. Chairman," said Charles Hardy.

Frank nodded to him to indicate that he had the floor.

" I move that a committee of three be appointed to draft and report a constitution for the club."

" Second the motion," added Sam Harper.

The motion prevailed. Charles Hardy, Tony Weston, and Fred Harper were nominated " at large," and chosen to serve on this committee. Leaving the hall, they retired to the boat room for deliberation; but the constitution had already been prepared by Frank and Charles, with the assistance of Captain Sedley. To make the business look more important and dignified, Charles insisted on remaining out a few moments, during which time they talked over the matter with Uncle Ben.

When they returned, the constitution was duly reported, and adopted, article by article.

Perhaps my young readers would not readily appreciate the moral of my story without reading this important document; therefore I add, in full, the

CONSTITUTION.

ARTICLE I.

This association shall be called the Zephyr Boat Club.

ARTICLE II.

The objects of the association shall be the instruction and amusement of the members, and the acquiring of good morals, good manners, and good habits in general.

Article III.

The officers of the club shall consist of a coxswain, or president, and a clerk.

Article IV.

It shall be the duty of the coxswain to command the boat, to preside at the meetings of the club, and to exercise a general supervision over its affairs. He shall hold his office for two weeks.

Article V.

The clerk shall keep a record of the meetings, and of all business pertaining to the club, and shall hold his office for four weeks.

Article VI.

No member of this club shall use profane language at any time. No member shall neglect his school, or his duties at home. No member shall use vulgar or indecent language. No member shall provoke a quarrel with another person, but shall do all he can to prevent fighting and unkindly feelings one to

wards another. No member shall use tobacco, or
ardent spirits as a beverage, in any form. All members shall obey the coxswain while in the boat. Any
member offending against either of the requirements
of this article, shall be liable to suspension, and if
incorrigible, to expulsion from the club.

Article VII.

In order the more perfectly to carry out the beneficent and reformatory purposes of the founder of
the club, to whose bounty we are indebted for the
opportunities of instruction and amusement the association affords us, we appoint him our director. All
violations of Article VI., and all violations of the
spirit of our organization, set forth in Article II.,
whether in word or in deed, shall be reported to our
director, and the delinquent shall be subject to such
penalty as he shall determine.

Article VIII.

The hall and library shall be open every Wednesday and Saturday afternoon, and every evening till
nine o'clock.

ARTICLE IX.

This constitution may be altered or amended by a vote of two thirds of the members.

This constitution was transferred to the record book, and duly signed. Some other business was transacted, and the meeting adjourned.

"Put on your uniforms," said Frank, as he rose from his chair, "and we will make our first appearance."

"At twelve o'clock there will be a collation ready for you on Centre Island," said Captain Sedley.

"Hurrah!" shouted Charles Hardy, as he rushed into the boat room.

CHAPTER XII.

THE "THUNDERBOLT."

THE appearance of the club in uniform was unique and pleasing, and each of the members was "every inch a sailor." Uncle Ben was delighted with the change, "they looked so much more shipshape than in their shore togs."

"Come, Uncle Ben, we are all ready," said Frank.

"I arn't goin' with you this time."

"You must go without him to-day, Frank," added Captain Sedley. "Uncle Ben must take the things over to the island for the collation."

"Are we to go alone?"

"Certainly."

"Hurrah!" cried Charles, who always used this word to express his gratification.

"But, boys, you must preserve good discipline. According to the constitution you must all obey the coxswain. And, Frank, be very careful; don't get aground on the rocks at the north shore, and if you go down the river, don't go too near the dam."

"I will not, father," replied Frank, who was fully impressed by the responsibility of his position as commander of the Zephyr. "Take your places in the boat. Tony, number them."

The doors which gave egress from the boat house to the lake were thrown open by Uncle Ben.

"Now, back her steady," continued Frank, standing up in the stern sheets. "Don't let her rub, Tony. Steady; one hard push; now she goes;" and the Zephyr shot out into the lake.

"The flags, Frank," said Charles.

"Ay, ay; Tony, hoist yours;" and at the same time, Frank raised the American flag at the stern.

"Ready; now for the oars. Up!"

"Down."

"Ready."

"Pull."

Frank felt like a prince as the Zephyr darted away.

"Where are you going, Frank?" asked Charles.

"I don't know; any where that the club wish to go."

13

" Up to Squaw Rock," suggested one.

" Down to Rippleton," said another.

" Over to the sawmill," added a third.

" Rest ! " cried Frank. " Lay on your oars, and we will decide it."

" What do you say to circumnavigating the lake ? " said Fred Harper.

" So I say," cried several.

" Those in favor of going round the lake say, ' Ay.' "

" Ay," shouted a large majority.

" Round it is," said Frank. " Pull ! "

Taking a course in the direction of Rippleton Village, Frank kept the boat as near the shore as her safety would permit. The boys rowed with remarkable precision, but with a very slow and measured stroke, so as to reserve their strength for the long pull before them.

" I wonder where the Bunkers are," said Charles.

" They haven't been seen on their raft for several days."

" I suppose they got sick of it when they saw the Zephyr."

"Very likely; their old raft didn't look much like our craft, when we went round them the other day."

Charles laughed at the contrast.

"What do you say to landing at Rippleton?" suggested he, as they approached the outlet of the lake.

"What for?" asked Frank.

"They haven't seen our new uniform down here."

"I think we had better not."

"Why not, Frank? Let us march through the streets, and get up a sensation."

"I would rather not. Some accident might happen to the boat while we are gone."

"O, nonsense!"

"Suppose the Bunkers should happen to see it?"

"They wouldn't dare to touch it."

"I am afraid they would."

"If I was coxswain, I would let you land," said Charles, sulkily.

"That isn't fair," said Tony.

"Humph!" sneered Charles.

"Don't get cross, Charley," interposed Frank.

"Who's cross?" said Charles, throwing down his oar.

"Mutiny!" laughed Fred Harper.

"Well, I ain't a-going to be snubbed round in that way."

"Charley, I haven't said a word that you need take offence at," said Frank, in a conciliatory tone.

"That he hasn't," interposed several.

"Yes, you have; and you needn't think you are going to tyrannize over me in that way."

"Pull steady," said Frank, calmly, as he put the helm hard up.

The boat came round in a graceful circle, and to the surprise of all, the coxswain headed her directly for the boat house.

"I thought you were going round the lake," said Sam Harper.

"Not now," replied Frank, quietly.

The boys pulled in silence for several minutes, and Charles Hardy leaned over the gunwale, and moodily watched the ripples on the side of the boat. He was conscious that he was introducing dissension into the club; but it seemed to him that Frank was ill natured in not gratifying him when he proposed to land at Rippleton.

The Zephyr was rapidly approaching the boat house, and Frank was sweeping her round so as to run her into the slip. The consequences of his behavior occurred to him. The provisions of article six of the constitution, and the penalty, came to his mind with appalling force. His conduct would be immediately reported to the director, and probably he would be suspended, or expelled from the club. He could not bear to think of such a thing.

The boat in a minute more would shoot into the boat house, and it would be too late to apologize. He could not endure the idea of " giving up," and owning that he was in the wrong; but to be suspended or expelled was a more bitter reflection.

" Frank," said he, in a gentle, insinuating tone.

" Rest!" cried the coxswain, promptly; " back her!"

" Forgive me, Frank," said the rebellious oarsman.

" You are rather late, Charley; but better late than never. We are almost into the boat house."

" I won't give you any more trouble — I solemnly

13 *

promise it, if you won't say any thing about it this time."

" According to the constitution, your conduct must be reported."

" Let him slide, this time," interposed Fred Harper.

" I freely forgive the offence, so far as I am concerned."

" Your father won't say any thing."

" He must know it," said Frank, firmly.

" What is the matter, boys ? " called Captain Sedley from the shore.

" Now, we are in for it ! " said Fred.

Charles Hardy hung his head with shame. Gladly would he have recalled his hasty words of anger; but it was too late. They had been spoken, and he must abide the consequences.

" Pull ! " said Frank, sadly, for he would fain have avoided the explanation which his father demanded.

The oarsmen pulled, and the boat was run into the house.

" Keep your places," said Frank, as he leaped out of the boat, and hastened to meet his father.

Captain Sedley was much astonished when he heard the story of Charles's sulkiness, and insisted that he should come ashore; but Frank pleaded for him, and the director finally consented, as it was the first offence under the new constitution, to pardon it.

Frank, delighted with his success, returned to the boat. Giving the necessary orders, the Zephyr shot out from her berth, and he steered, as before, towards Rippleton. Charles was deeply mortified when he reflected upon his quarrelsome behavior, and mentally resolved never to be guilty of such conduct again. But he was anxious to know what disposition Captain Sedley had made of his case, and whether he should be held to answer for his disobedience when they went ashore. He did not like to say any thing about it, though, at first; but after more reflection, his better nature overcame his pride.

"Frank," said he, with a smile.

"Well, Charley."

"I am sorry for what I did."

"I knew you were, and for that reason I begged my father to excuse it, and have nothing more said about it.'

" You are too generous, Frank ; I don't deserve it of you."

" It was an offence against the club, more than against me," replied Frank.   " I am glad you think better of it."

" I never will do it again."

" I hope not, Charley.   You know the constitution provides for a new coxswain every two weeks ; when you are chosen, I shall obey your orders."

" I don't deserve to be coxswain."

" Well, never mind it.   It is all right now."

Good feeling was again restored, and the boys once more began to enjoy themselves.   The Zephyr worked admirably, and Frank deported himself with so much dignity and firmness, that the boys rendered the most unqualified obedience to all his orders. But he was not tyrannical or overbearing.   When there was a difference of opinion, he was always ready to yield his own inclination to the wishes of the majority.

The boat passed round the lower end of the lake, and was approaching its upper extremity.

" What's that ? " exclaimed Frank, rising from his

seat, as he discovered a boat lying near the shore
full of boys.

"Rest!" said he.

"It is the Bunkers," said Tony. "I see Tim in
the stern."

"It is Joe Braman's boat," added Fred Harper.
"Here they come."

"Twig the flags!" cried Charles Hardy.

"In imitation of the Zephyr," said Frank, laughing heartily.

The boat approached near enough for them to examine her. It was, as Fred had declared, Joe Braman's boat; but she had been very much altered.
Apparently she had been sawed in two and lengthened out. She had been painted bright yellow, with
a red streak round her, and on the bows, after the
manner of the Zephyr, was inscribed, in black letters,
the name "Thunderbolt," which was in accordance
with Tim Bunker's taste. She was pulled by eight
oars, and the redoubtable leader of the gang sat in
the stern sheets as coxswain. Forward floated a
blue cotton rag, with the letter T daubed upon it in
white paint, and surrounded by half a dozen ill-

shaped stars.   At the stern was a ragged piece of bunting, which had once been the flag of the republic, but which had been curtailed of nine of its stripes and a part of its stars.

The Bunkers evidently had not practised rowing much, for their stroke was irregular, and they splashed the water about like so many porpoises.   Occasionally one of them got hit in the back by his neighbor's oar, which produced a great deal of swearing and wrangling among them.   They made but slow progress through the water, and the Zephyrs could scarcely refrain from laughing at the singular spectacle.

CHAPTER XIII.

THE COLLISION.

JOE BRAMAN, the alleged proprietor of the Thunderbolt, was an idle, dissolute fellow, who employed his time in gunning, fishing, and loitering about the dramshops of Rippleton. He lived in a miserable hut on the north shore of the lake. How he obtained his living, it would have been difficult to determine.

Tim Bunker was an especial favorite with Braman, and people said it was because there was a natural sympathy between them. Joe's boat was a long, flat-bottomed affair, not very graceful in its form or construction. With the exception of Captain Sedley's sailboat, and the club boat, it was, perhaps, the only boat on the lake; and small parties occasionally engaged Joe to take them out fishing in it.

The history of its present appearance was sufficiently plain to the Zephyrs. It had been lengthened out, painted, a sharp, false bow attached to it, and such other improvements made as would fit it for the purposes of a club boat.

"Isn't she one of the boats?" laughed Charles.

"Silence, forward!" said Frank, shaking his head as a gesture of warning to the boys not to provoke any ill nature.

"Who you lookin' at!" cried Tim Bunker, as the Thunderbolt came near the Zephyr.

"Good morning, Tim," said Frank, pleasantly.

"Why don't you pull, you lubbers?" shouted Tim.

"You have a new boat, I see."

"I'll bet we have," replied Tim, bringing the Thunderbolt round the stern of the Zephyr.

"Isn't that Joe Braman's boat?" asked Charles.

"No, sir-ee! It's my boat," answered Tim.

"Did you buy it of him?"

"Didn't do nothin' else."

"What did you give?"

"Ten dollars, and five for fixin' her up," replied Tim, with a great deal of importance.

"She looks very well," continued Charles.

"She'll go some, you better believe."

Tony Weston could not help smiling at this conversation, and Tim Bunker unfortunately perceived the funny expression on his face. It roused his anger.

"Who stole the wallet?" said he.

This taunt roused a feeling of indignation in the soul of Fred Harper, and he so far forgot the requirements of the constitution as to reply, —

"Tim Bunker."

"Le's lick 'em," said one of the Bunkers.

"Pull!" exclaimed Frank, with energy, when he saw the storm brewing.

Mindful of the discipline of the club, every member obeyed the order, and the Zephyr darted away from the belligerent Thunderbolts.

"Pooh! Frank, I wouldn't run away fiom them," said Charles.

"I have no desire to quarrel with such fellows," replied Frank; "and I hope none of you will say any thing to provoke them. That was very thoughtless of you, Fred."

"I know it; but, somehow, I couldn't help it;

14

the taunt was so mean and contemptible. If I had been on shore, I should have knocked him."

"Article six," said Frank.

"Here they come after us," added Tony.

The boys all laughed involuntarily at the idea of the old "gundalow," as Fred called it, chasing them.

"They can't catch us," continued Frank.

"I guess not," said Charles.

"But I am sorry we provoked them, for I had a little plan in my head."

"What is it, Frank?"

"Never mind it now; rest on your oars; we are a quarter of a mile from them, and we can easily keep out of their way."

"Steady, Frank, we are running too near the shore," interposed Tony. "The water is shoal here, you know."

"Back her!" exclaimed the coxswain. "I was watching the Bunkers so closely that I did not mind where we were going. Back her, quick!"

But it was too late. The Zephyr darted forward, and buried her keel in the mud at the bottom of the lake.

" By gracious ! " exclaimed Charles Hardy; " we are in for it now."

" And the Bunkers are upon us," added Frank, very much perplexed by the difficulties which had so suddenly surrounded them.

" What shall be done ? " asked Tony.

" Let them come on," replied Fred. " We can't get rid of them now."

" I don't want to fight with them."

The Thunderbolt was approaching them, not very rapidly, it was true ; but a few minutes would involve them in a quarrel, which Frank and a large majority of the club were very anxious to avoid. Tim Bunker was standing up in the stern sheets of his boat, watching them with malignant interest.

" Hurrah ! they are aground ! " cried Tim, as soon as he understood the nature of the calamity which had befallen the Zephyr. " We have them now; they can't run away, the cowardly long faces ! "

" Come aft, some of you," said Frank, when he heard these threatening words. " The water is deep enough under the stern. We have only run into a mud bank."

On the starboard side of the boat there was plenty of water, and if they could move her back a rod, they could easily escape.

The boys obeyed the order of the coxswain; but the Zephyr had been forced so deeply into the mud that her bow still stuck fast.

"Half a dozen of you, set your oars in the mud, and push!" continued Frank, highly excited by the danger that menaced them.

But it was of no use; they could not start her.

"They are upon us," said Tony.

"What shall we do?" asked Frank, sadly perplexed.

"We must fight," said Fred.

"No, I am not willing to do that."

"Shall we sit here and let them pound us as much as they have a mind to?" replied Fred. "But you are coxswain, Frank, and I, for one, shall do just what you say."

"So shall I!" said another.

"And I!"

And so they all said.

Frank was more and more embarrassed as the

circumstances multiplied the difficulties around him. He was charged with the direction of the whole club, and the responsibility of his position rested heavily upon his mind. He had been taught at the fireside of his pious home to avoid a quarrel at almost any sacrifice ; and he was painfully conscious that the indiscreet words of Fred Harper had provoked the anger of the Bunkers. Poor fellow! What could he do ? He could not order them to fight, not even in self-defence, under the circumstances, and he knew that their foes would whip them severely if they did not. The Thunderbolt was within a few rods of them, and five minutes more would decide the question.

" We are in a bad fix ! " said Charles, nervously " What are you going to do, Frank ? "

" Tony, take your boathook, and see how deep the water is on the mud bank."

" Only about a foot," replied Tony, as he obeyed the order.

" Is the mud deep ? "

" Not very," replied Tony, pushing the boathook down.

14*

" I want two volunteers," said Frank, hurriedly,

" I ! " cried Tony.

" I ! " repeated half a dozen others.

" Tony and Fred ; throw off your pants and jump into the water.   You can easily push her off."

" Agreed ! " cried the two volunteers, as they hastened to execute the order.

" Six of you take your oars ; back her as they push ; the other four stay in the stern sheets to settle her down aft."

" Ay, ay ! " exclaimed the boys.

" Now for it !   Pull ! "

The effect was instantly perceived ; the boat was moved back about a foot.

" Once more, all together ! " said Frank.

Another effort backed her about two feet more, and the case began to look hopeful.

" Again, quick ! they are upon us ! Leap in, Tony and Fred, when she is free."

" Heave again ! " said Tony.

Their exertions were now crowned with entire success, and the Zephyr darted back into deep water ; but an unfortunate occurrence rendered all their labor futile. As the boat slid off the mud bank, Tony and Fred, in their attempt to spring on board, embarrassed each other's movements, so that the former lost his hold, and remained standing up to his middle in the mud and water.

At this instant the Thunderbolt reached the spot, and Tim steered directly for poor Tony, whose situation he discovered the moment the Zephyr was free.

" Hit him ! " screamed Tim. " Pound him with your oars ! Drownd him ! "

Frank's blood seemed to freeze in his veins, as he perceived the imminent peril of his friend. He knew the Bunkers would not spare him, and that even his life was in danger.

Fortunately the Thunderbolt grounded, or Tony would inevitably have been borne under her bottom. Tim seized an oar, and with the ferocity of a madman, sprang forward to execute his vengeance on the helpless boy.

" Let him alone ! " shouted Frank, with frantic earnestness. " Man your oars, boys ! Ready — pull ! "

Frank was fully roused, and his orders were delivered with rapidity and energy. Seizing the tiller ropes, he steered the boat, as she gathered headway, so that her sharp bow struck the Thunderbolt on her broadside, staving in her gunwale and upsetting her.

The Bunkers thought this was rather sharp practice, as they floundered about in the water. They had not given Frank Sedley credit for half so much determination. They had never seen any thing in him that betokened "spunk" before. He was a peaceable boy, always avoiding a quarrel; but when the very life of his friend was in peril, he was found to be as bold and courageous as the best of them.

The bow of the Zephyr was swung round so that Tony could get in. Washing off the mud from his legs, he resumed his dress.

In the mean time the Bunkers had righted their boat and resumed their places. The bath they had had quite cooled their belligerent heat; though, if it had not, Frank had taken the precaution to back the Zephyr out of their reach.

"You'll catch it for this!" exclaimed Tim Bunker,

as his crew were bailing out the Thunderbolt with their hats.

" I am sorry for what has happened, Tim," replied Frank, " but I could not help it."

" Couldn't help it, you —— " I will not soil the pages of my book by writing the expression that Tim made use of. " Yes, yer could help it. What d'yer run inter me for? "

" You threatened to drown Tony, and if your boat had not got aground you would have run him down."

" That I would, long face ! If ever I catch either of you, I will lick yer within an inch of yer life — mind that ! "

" I am sorry for it, Tim."

" Yer lie, yer ain't ! "

" It was all my fault, Tim," interposed Fred, " and I will pay for the damage done your boat."

" I guess yer better." .

" How much will you take, and call it square ? "

" Dollar and a half," growled Tim, glancing at the fractured gunwale.

Fred had not so much money with him, but the sum was immediately raised in the club.

" Now, Tim, we will forget and forgive : what do you say ? "

" I don't want nothin' on yer ; give me the money, and I don't care what yer do."

Frank ordered the crew to pull up to the Thunderbolt, and Fred handed Tim the money.

" I'll pay yer for this ; see 'f I don't," said the unforgiving Bunker, as the Zephyr backed away.

CHAPTER XIV.

CENTRE ISLAND.

FRANK SEDLEY was very much disturbed by the events of the forenoon. His conscience assured him, however, that he had done nothing wrong. He had not tried to provoke a quarrel with the Bunkers, and the unpleasant occurrences of the past hour were wholly owing to their misfortune in getting aground. He would not have been justified, he felt, in leaving Tony at the mercy of his relentless foes.

Fred Harper had done wrong in replying to the taunt of Tim, and this would make a case for the decision of their director.

" We must keep away from them, hereafter," said he, as the Zephyr came about, and the crew commenced rowing again.

" That will be the best way," added Tony.

" So I think," said Charles : " we shall be all the time getting into scrapes, if we go near them."

"We can go near them without meddling," interposed Fred Harper.

"But, Fred, you remember what made all the fuss."

"It was my fault, I know."

"I don't want to be hard with you while I am coxswain, but if any member says or does any thing, while we are on the lake, to get us into a scrape, I shall consider it my duty to land him immediately at the boat house. What do you say to that?"

No boy spoke for a moment; but at last Tony said, —

"That would be perfectly fair."

"I want to have it understood," continued Frank. "My father will not let us come out alone again, if we are likely to have such a time as this."

"Why need you tell him any thing about it, Frank?" asked Charles.

"Because it is right that he should know it. Suppose we should conceal it, and then he should find it out?"

"That would only make a bad matter worse," replied Tony.

"For one, I am satisfied to have any fellow that tries to get us into a scrape put ashore," said Fred Harper.

"So am I," added Tony.

All the rest of the club expressed themselves willing to comply with this arrangement.

"Now, be careful, all of you," continued Frank, "and we shall have no more trouble."

"But while the Bunkers are on the lake, we can't help meeting them once in a while," said one.

"We need not say any thing to them."

"But that would not be civil."

"We can answer them kindly, if they say any thing to us."

"They won't forget the smash up."

"We can easily keep out of their way."

"Where are you going now, Frank?"

"Isn't it almost twelve?"

"Half past eleven," returned Fred Harper, who carried a watch. "You said you had a plan, Frank."

"I was thinking of asking Mrs. Weston and Mary to take a sail with us."

15

" Good ! " replied half a dozen voices.

" We will take them over to the island."

The proposition was agreed to, and Frank steered the boat into the little cove near the widow Weston's cottage.

" Tony and Charles shall be a committee to go and invite them," said Frank, as the bow of the Zephyr touched the land.

The two jumped ashore to discharge the duty assigned them.

" Where's the Thunderbolt ? " asked Fred, rising from his seat.

" There she goes over to the north shore."

" Putting in to repair damages."

" Where do you suppose Tim got the money to buy that boat with ? " said Fred, looking seriously at Frank.

" I don't know," replied the latter ; but a gleam of intelligence penetrated his mind. " I hadn't thought of it before."

" I don't know, either, but I can guess."

" You might guess wrong."

" Fifteen dollars is a great deal of money for a

boy like him to have. His father works in one of the mills at Rippleton."

" Here comes Tony with his sister."

" Where is your mother, Tony ? "

" She couldn't go, but she said Mary might."

" Stop a moment, Tony, and we will bring the stern round by that rock," said Frank. " Ready with your oars — back her ! That will do ; now pull on the larboard and back the starboard oars — steady."

The stern of the Zephyr came up to the rock, and the gallant coxswain assisted Mary to a seat by his side. Tony and Charles resumed their places at the oars.

" How pretty your boat is ! " exclaimed Mary, delighted with the appearance of the Zephyr.

" Very pretty indeed. Ready — pull."

" But won't it tip over ? " cried Mary, as the boat darted out of the cove.

" O, no ; there is not the least danger."

" And you guide it with those strings ? " asked the wondering girl.

" Yes ; they are fastened to that crosspiece, you see, and when I pull them, it moves the rudder."

" What is the rudder, Frank ? "

" You can see only the upper end of it ; but it is a flat piece of wood, which acts upon the water and turns the boat," replied the obliging coxswain, illustrating his explanation by means of his hands.

" O my ! how swift it goes ! "

" Not very fast now."

" Why, it goes like a race horse."

The boys smiled at Mary's enthusiasm.

" Let her drive a little, Frank," suggested Fred Harper.

Frank commenced swaying his body back and forth, increasing in rapidity till the boys put forth their utmost exertion. Mary held on to the gunwale of the boat, as her speed augmented, and she seemed almost to fly through the water.

" Isn't it beautiful ! " exclaimed Mary.

Frank was so intent upon the movements of the excited crew, that he scarcely noticed they had nearly reached the north shore.

" There ! that will do ; rest," said he.

" I should think they would be very tired," added Mary.

" Perhaps they are ; we came over very quick ; the distance is nearly two miles."

" Twig the Bunkers ! " said Charles.

The Zephyr was within a short distance of the landing in front of Joe Braman's house. The Thunderbolt had just put in there, and as they approached Joe and Tim were examining the nature of the damages their boat had sustained.

" What does he say, Tony ? " asked Fred.

" He says he can easily fix it."

" Pull," said Frank. " Row very slowly."

Steering the boat round by Joe Braman's landing, they saw Joe go into the house, and return with a hammer and some nails, with which he proceeded to nail a piece of board over the fracture in the side of the Thunderbolt.

" I can't fix it any better to-day ; I'm going to Boston in the two o'clock train."

" Will that hold ? " asked Tim.

" Yes ; she won't leak. Now just row me over to Rippleton."

" There is the villains of long faces," said Tim, pointing at the Zephyr. " Jump in, fellers, and

15 *

just throw some of them stones into the boat. We'll give it to 'em yet."

" Joe's going to Boston," said Fred.

" So he says."

The Bunkers threw the stones into their boat, and then got in themselves. In imitation of the discipline of the Zephyr, the oars were first placed in a perpendicular position, and then dropped into the water.

" Pull," said Tim, steering directly towards the Zephyr.

" Most twelve," suggested Fred Harper, with a significant glance at Frank.

" Pull," replied the latter, smiling.

" Want to race ? " shouted Tim.

" With the greatest pleasure."

" Come alongside, then, and we will take a fair start."

" No, you don't ! " said Frank, in a low tone, apprehending an attack from his quarrelsome rival. " I will give you twenty rods the start," continued he, aloud.

" You darsent come," sneered Tim.

Joe Braman was seen to speak to Tim, and instantly the Thunderbolt was headed towards the Zephyr.

"Pull with all your might!" cried the Bunker.

"Drive 'em into that 'ere cove, and then you can fix 'em," said Joe.

But Frank gave the cove a "wide berth." A very little exertion on the part of the club was sufficient to keep them out of the reach of the Bunkers, and they continued their course leisurely towards Centre Island.

Joe Braman saw that the chase was hopeless, and at his suggestion, the Thunderbolt abandoned the pursuit, and steered towards Rippleton.

"Those are dreadful bad boys," said Mary Weston, when, to her intense relief, she saw them give up the chase.

"That they are; but our boat is so much swifter than theirs that we can easily keep out of their way."

"Do you suppose they really meant to stone you?"

"I have no doubt of it."

"Nearly twelve," said Fred Harper, looking at **his** watch.

"Give way, my lads; we will be there in time."

The clock on the distant church was striking twelve when they touched at the island. The Zephyr was turned round and backed in shore, so that Mary could land conveniently.

"How do you do, Mary? I am glad to see you," said Captain Sedley, as he helped her on shore. "And, Frank, your mother is coming over. The wind was so light, we could not sail. Will you row her over?"

"O, yes, father."

"I suppose you are more ready and willing than the boys who pull the boat."

"We are all ready and willing," shouted the boys.

"Hurrah! so we are," added Charles Hardy.

"She is waiting in the boat house."

The Zephyr pushed off again, and in a very few minutes returned with Mrs. Sedley as passenger. Frank was delighted to show his mother how skilful the club had become, and she was much pleased with her excursion.

Uncle Ben secured the boat to a tree, and the boys all landed. Every thing was ready for their reception. The table, which was covered with every description of "nice things," was laid under the shade of a tall oak in the miniature forest.

Captain Sedley sat at one end and Uncle Ben at the other. Mrs. Sedley and Mary were on the right. The director prefaced the entertainment with a few remarks, and then invited them to do justice to the feast that was set before them.

"All ready!" exclaimed Captain Sedley, with a loud voice.

The boys all wondered what made him speak so very loud ; and Frank perceived a mysterious smile on the lips of his mother, and he was quite sure it meant something.

Suddenly, and to the intense surprise of all the boys, a band, which had been stationed in the grove near them, struck up Hail Columbia.

"Hurrah!" cried Charles Hardy, in a burst of enthusiastic delight.

The music was an unexpected treat, and as the Rippleton Brass Band poured forth its most inspiring strains, there were no bounds to the delight of the boys. But the music did not prevent their doing ample justice to the viands set before them.

After the collation was finished, Frank told his father all the circumstances of their morning excursion. Captain Sedley did not blame Fred very much for the taunt he had used, considering the provocation. He was satisfied that the boat club organization would correct such indiscretions in due time. He decided, however, that Fred should submit to some penalty, to be affixed at another time, and that Frank was right in not leaving Tony at the mercy of the Bunkers.

Frank continued his story, and incidentally remarked that the Bunkers had just rowed Joe Braman to Rippleton, where he intended to take the cars for Boston.

Captain Sedley mused a moment.

"The cars start at two o'clock," said he, consulting his watch. "Boys, I must go to Boston, and you must row me down to the village as quick as you can."

" Zephyrs, ahoy ! " shouted Frank.

The club were in their seats in a moment, and the Zephyr darted away towards Rippleton.

CHAPTER XV.

GEOGRAPHY OF WOOD LAKE.

CAPTAIN SEDLEY reached the depot just in time to take the two o'clock train, and the club returned to Centre Island, where another hour was spent very pleasantly in listening to the music of the band, and in such amusements as the ingenuity of boys can devise.

But at last they grew tired of the land. The beautiful Zephyr, resting so lightly and gracefully on the water, seemed to invite them to more congenial sports.

"Mother, won't you let us row you round the lake?" asked Frank. "We want to go on an exploring voyage."

"With pleasure; but the band is engaged for all the afternoon."

"Can't we take them in the boat?"

"I'm afraid it is not large enough; there are thirteen musicians."

"That would be first rate — music on the water!" exclaimed Charles Hardy.

"What do you think, Uncle Ben?" asked Mrs. Sedley.

"I don't think it would be safe, marm."

"I am afraid not."

"O, yes, it would!" cried Charles, disappointed at the thought of resigning the plan.

"There is not room enough in the Zephyr for them. But there's a little breeze springing up, and I'll take them in the sail boat."

"That will do just as well," replied Mrs. Sedley.

"But you can't keep up with us, Uncle Ben," said Charles.

"Then you must go slower."

"Zephyrs, ahoy!" cried Frank.

The club hastened to the boat, and seated themselves. The musicians found ample room in the large sail boat.

"Stop a minute, mother, till we go about and

16

bring the stern in shore," said Frank, as he gave the word to elevate the oars.

Uncle Ben and his party had already got under way, and the band commenced playing Wood Up, as the sail boat slowly gathered headway.

The Zephyr backed in, and Mrs. Sedley and Mary Weston were assisted to their seats by the gallant young coxswain.

"Pull steady," said Frank, as the club boat shot out from the land.

"How fine the music sounds on the water!" said Mary.

"Beautiful," replied Mrs. Sedley. "I am sorry your mother is not with us, Mary."

"She could not come before dinner."

"Would she join us now, do you think?"

"I guess she would."

"We can go and see, at any rate," said Frank. "Uncle Ben is steering that way."

"Do, Frank; I have something I wish to say to her."

"Bunkers!" exclaimed Fred Harper.

"Where?"

" Coming up from Rippleton."

" I hope they will keep away from us," added Frank, whose forenoon experience was still remembered.

" They will want to hear the music."

" You must keep near Uncle Ben, Frank."

The Zephyr was rapidly approaching the Sylph, as the sail boat was called.

" I wish they would play Old Folks at Home," said Charles.

" We can ask them to do so," replied Mrs. Sedley.

Suddenly Frank stood up in his place.

" Rest," said he, with a smile.

" What are you going to do ? " asked his mother.

" I am going to execute a manœuvre ; and, boys, I want you to be prompt in your movements."

" Ay, ay ! " shouted the club.

" Now, then, pull ! "

Frank swayed his body for a few moments with great rapidity, and of course, the stroke of the rowers corresponded to his motions. The Zephyr darted forward with a speed which surprised Mrs. Sedley.

" Rest ! " cried Frank, when the boat came within a few rods of the Sylph.

" Be careful, my son ; you will run against her," interposed Mrs. Sedley, as she involuntarily grasped the gunwale of the boat.

The dripping oars were all extended at the same height from the water, at the command of the coxswain.

" Up ! " continued he.

" You will certainly run against them, Frank," repeated Mrs. Sedley.   " Pray don't be careless."

" There is nothing to fear, mother."

Indeed the Zephyr was approaching fearfully near the Sylph, and even Uncle Ben began to feel a little uneasy.

" Port your helm, Frank ! " shouted the veteran.

" Keep her steady, Uncle Ben."

Frank, looking through the two rows of perpendicular oars, steered the Zephyr alongside her companion, and passed within a very few inches of her.

" Play Old Folks at Home, if you please," said he, as the boat darted by the sluggish Sylph.

"That was a little too close, my son," said Mrs Sedley.

"We are perfectly safe, mother, are we not?"

"We are; but, Frank, you should never expose yourself, and especially not others, to needless peril."

"We were in no danger."

"I think you were."

"The Zephyr is under perfect control; she feels the slightest turn of the rudder."

"Suppose Uncle Ben's boat had swerved a little from her course?"

"There was no fear of that."

"You do not know. If it had, we might have been drowned, many of us, at least."

Frank looked serious.

"Ask Uncle Ben what he thinks about it."

"Down!" said Frank.

The boys commenced pulling again, and the coxswain steered so as to bring the Zephyr in a circle round the Sylph.

"Now we will keep alongside, but at a safe distance," said he, as he laid her course parallel with that of his companion.

16 *

The band were preparing to play the tune which Frank had requested. The Sylph was making very good progress through the water, and the rowers kept pulling with a very slow stroke.

"You were careless, Frank," said Uncle Ben, when the band stopped playing.

"Do you think so, Uncle Ben?"

"Very careless; in the navy they would have put you in irons for it. There arn't no need of risking the lives of your crew in that way. If it had been to save the life of a feller creter, or any thing of that sort, there would have been some sense in it."

"I didn't think there was any danger," returned Frank not a little troubled by the veteran's censure.

"I'm sailin' right afore the wind, you see, and the boat swings fore and aft, like a French dancing master. If she had a swayed only a leetle grain, we might all have gone to the bottom."

"I never will be so careless again."

"You were all-fired careless, Frank," said Charles Hardy.

Fred Harper could not help turning round and

looking the speaker full in the face, to reprove him for his interference.

Frank felt the rebuke of his friend, and was not a little hurt by the reproach, coming as it did from one whom he had used with so much lenity — for whom he had so strenuously interceded with his father.

" Hush up ! Charley," said Fred, in a low tone. " Don't you know any better than that ? "

The band now struck up Old Folks at Home.

" Let us sing," said Frank.

" So I say," replied Tony.

" Wait till they come to the chorus," added Fred.

At the right moment the boys commenced the chorus, and the effect was very pleasing. Mrs. Sedley and Mary's voices were heard with the others, and all were delighted.

" Here's the cove," said Frank, when the band ceased playing. " We were going on a voyage of discovery this afternoon, to name the bays and points of land. What shall we call this cove ? "

" Weston Bay," suggested Fred.

" Agreed ! " answered a dozen members.

" And that mud bank over there, where we **got**

aground this morning, we will call Bunker's Shoal,"
continued Fred.

"I think not," said Mrs. Sedley. "That would
be casting a reflection upon those boys."

"What shall we call it?"

"Black Shoal," replied Tony. "The mud on it,
I know from personal experience, is very black."

"Black Shoal it is," replied Frank, directing the
boat into the little bay. "Pull lively."

The invitation of Mrs. Sedley was quite sufficient
to induce Mrs. Weston to join the "exploring expedition," and the committee that had been deputed to
wait upon her soon returned, escorting her to the
boat.

"Dear me! won't it tip over?" exclaimed the
poor woman, when she had placed one foot in the
boat.

"She is perfectly safe," replied Frank, assisting
her to a seat.

The boat pushed off again, and joined the Sylph.
The band commenced playing a popular march, and
all the party, with the exception of Mrs. Weston,
who had her suspicions as to the stability of the

beautiful Zephyr, were in the highest state of enjoyment.

Farther up the lake there was a projecting headland, at the end of which, separated from the shore
by a narrow passage of water, not more than ten
feet in width, was a small, rocky island. This island
and its vicinity were the next points of interest de-
serving the attention of the voyagers, and thither
Frank steered the boat.

"Boys, you all study geography, do you not?"
asked Mrs. Sedley.

"All of us, mother," replied Frank.

"Did it ever occur to you that all the natural
divisions of water, on a small scale, could be seen in
Wood Lake?"

"Can they?" asked Charles. "I would not have
believed it."

"I never thought of it before," added Frank.

"Years ago, before I was married, I used to teach
school," continued Mrs. Sedley; "and my scholars
always found it difficult to remember the definitions
of the natural divisions of the earth. What do you
think the reason was?"

"I suppose they did not half learn them," replied Fred.

"They did not understand them. When we spoke of a gulf, for example, they thought of something a great way off — as far as the Gulf of Mexico, or the Gulf of St. Lawrence."

"I am sure I never thought of them as any thing that I had ever seen, or was ever likely to see," added Charles, who always had something to say, and who tried to get the good will of others by appearing to be humble and teachable.

The other boys were equally tractable, but from another motive. Mrs. Sedley's geography lesson was full of interest to them, and as they pulled slowly, they gave all their attention to what she said.

"I took them out one day to a pond near the school house, where I pointed out almost all the divisions of water, and then on a hill, to show them the divisions of land."

"But you could not find them all."

"All but one or two ; there was no volcano."

"Was there a desert?"

"A small one."

"Hurrah! we can find them all," cried Charles. "I missed just such a question last week in school."

"I made a volcano on the fourth of July," said Fred Harper.

"Indeed! how?"

"I took a handful of powder, wet it, and then placed it on a board. Then I covered it over with a coat of wet clay, leaving a little hole at the top, with some dry powder on it."

"That was the crater," added Charles.

"Yes; and then I touched it off. It was in the evening, and it looked just like Mount Vesuvius in the panorama."

"Now, boys," continued Mrs. Sedley, "who can tell me what an ocean is?"

"The largest body of water," replied several.

"What shall represent the ocean here?"

"The lake."

"Very well; what is a sea?"

"A portion of water smaller than an ocean, and nearly surrounded by land."

"We are in one now," said Frank.

He had steered the Zephyr into a corner of the

lake which was partly enclosed by the projecting headland and island, and the main shore.

"What sea shall we call it?" said Fred.

The boys looked around them for some object that would suggest a name.

CHAPTER XVI.

OVERBOARD!

THERE was no visible object which seemed to suggest a name for the miniature sea ; but just then the band began to play Washington's March.

" Call it Washington Sea, boys," said Mrs. Sedley.

The name was given ; but the geography lesson could not proceed while the music continued, and Frank ordered the boys to rest. The Bunkers, attracted by the music of the band, followed the Sylph at a respectful distance. The presence of Uncle Ben and Mrs. Sedley was a restraint upon them, and they conducted themselves with tolerable decorum. The band ceased playing, and Mrs. Sedley continued her instructions.

' What is a gulf or bay ? "

" A portion of the sea extending into the land."

" Can you give me an example ? "

" Weston Bay," replied Fred, laughing.

17

" And, perhaps, before the expedition concludes · its voyage, we shall find something which may be called a gulf."

" I know where there is a gulf," said Charles.

" Now, Frank, you may go through the straits."

" Is it safe ? I don't know how deep the water is."

" I am glad to see you are careful," said Mrs. Sedley. " You can ask Uncle Ben."

" Sylph, ahoy ! " shouted Frank, rising.

" What boat's that ? " roared Uncle Ben, in reply.

" The Zephyr, of and from Rippleton," returned the coxswain. " Can you tell me what depth of water there is in this passage ? "

" Where's your chart ? "

" We must have a chart of the lake," suggested Fred.

" That we must.   Who shall draw it ? "

" Fred Harper."

" We have no chart.   Will you give me the depth of water ? " continued Frank.

" Short fathom," replied Uncle Ben.

" We are none the wiser," interposed Charles. " How much is a fathom ? "

" Six feet," answered Tony.

" But he don't say how much short."

" Can we go through in safety, Uncle Ben ? "

" Ay, ay ; unship your oars first."

Frank let the crew pull several smart strokes, and then ordered the oars up. The Zephyr darted through the narrow passage.

" Now for the name of the strait," said Frank.

" You seem to be at a loss for names ; I think you had better call these divisions after the members of the club," suggested Mrs. Sedley.

" So we can ; the memory of great travellers and navigators has been handed down to their posterity by geographical names — Hudson Bay, Mount Franklin, Cook's Straits, for example," said Fred Harper, laughing heartily.

The proposition received a ready assent, and the strait was called Calrow Strait, after the boy who pulled the second oar.

" But the island ? " said Charles.

" Billy Curtis pulls the third oar ; we will call it Curtis Island."

The position of the boat was a favorable one for

observing the conformation of the country, and Mrs Sedley improved the opportunity to point out the various divisions of the land.

Half way between Centre Island and the north shore was another island; and after coasting along by the banks of the lake, applying names to miniature sounds, bays, gulfs, and seas, the Zephyr arrived at its southerly side.

"Here is a channel," said Frank; "a passage of water wider than a strait."

"Fred's turn; we must call it Harper Channel," replied Tony.

"And the island? — we are out of names," continued Frank.

"We will call it Mary's Island, after Mary Weston."

"Agreed!" cried a dozen boys at once.

"I thank you for the compliment," said Mary, blushing.

The excursion was continued, the boys rowing leisurely, and pausing frequently to listen to the music of the band, and discuss the geographical formation of the lake and its shores. They passed entirely round the lake, and had given so many names to the various divisions of land and water, that it seemed improbable they could ever remember them.

As they came round to the boat house, Mrs. Sedley was landed, and the club rowed up to Weston Bay, to leave the widow and her daughter. Both the passengers were delighted with their excursion, and were profuse of their thanks to Frank and his companions for their kindness and consideration.

"What shall we do now?" said Charles, as they pushed off.

"Hadn't we better give up for to-day?" suggested Frank.

"Let us go down to Rippleton for your father," added Fred.

"I will do that," answered Frank; and the Zephyr dashed away towards the village.

They had scarcely passed the boat house before they discovered the Thunderbolt, directly ahead of them. Uncle Ben had landed the band at Rippleton, and had housed the Sylph, so that the Bunkers would no longer be restrained by his presence and

17*

that of Mrs. Sedley. But there was no way to avoid them, and Frank continued his course with some misgivings as to the consequences.

" Bunkers ahead ! " said he.

" Never mind them, Frank," added Fred Harper. " We won't say any thing to them."

" Tim will get his revenge upon us for this morning if he can."

" We can keep out of his way, though I don't like the idea of running away from them."

" I like it better than I do the idea of fighting with them, But the lake is narrow near the village."

" We can row two rods to their one."

" They have improved a great deal by their day's practice. They are resting on their oars, waiting for us."

" Let them wait ; we will mind nothing about them."

The Zephyr continued on her course. It was necessary for her to pass within a short distance of the Thunderbolt, and Frank feared they would retaliate upon them for their discomfiture in the forenoon.

" Let every member of the club mind his oar,"

said he, as the boat approached the vicinity of the Bunkers; "I will watch them; I want you to mind what I say, and work quick when I speak."

"We will," answered the boys.

"I suspect, if they mean any thing, that they intend to rush upon us when we pass them. Yes, there is Tim bringing her head round so that she lies broadside to us, and every one of them has his oar ready to pull."

"Can't you cut across the lake, and avoid them?" asked Tony.

"We must pass them somewhere, and they can cut us off, whatever course we take."

"Smash them, if they come too near," said Fred.

"No, no, Fred; that wouldn't do. When I tell you to stop and back her, do it promptly, and we can easily get away from them. Pull steady."

The boys rowed leisurely, and the Zephyr in a short time reached a position which was exposed to the assault of the Thunderbolt.

"Pull!" cried Tim Bunker, with energy.

Her course was at right angles with that of the Zephyr. Tim had apparently made a nice calculation in regard to his intended movements. He had started so as to come up with his rival, when she came to the point in her course directly ahead of him.

The Bunkers pulled with all their might, and the two boats were rapidly nearing each other. Tim's plan had been well conceived, and the collision seemed inevitable. Frank saw that he had rightly interpreted the intentions of the Bunkers; but he still continued his course.

Suddenly, as the Thunderbolt was on the point of pouncing upon her prey, Frank, with startling energy, gave the command, —

"Stop, and back her!"

Every boy, expecting the order, was ready to execute it. The oars bent under the violent exertion they made to check the farther progress of the boat.

When the collision seemed unavoidable, Tim abandoned the helm, and leaped forward into the bow of the boat. He had a large stick in his hand, and it was evidently his intention to use it upon poor Tony, for his glance was fixed upon him with savage ferocity.

Frank's plan worked well. He had withheld the order to stop and back her till the last moment, so that Tim should have no time to change the course of the Thunderbolt, and thus derange his plan. As it was, it was a very narrow escape, and nothing but the promptness with which the order was executed averted the impending catastrophe.

The Thunderbolt passed across the course of the Zephyr, not three feet from her bow. Tim saw that he was foiled, and enraged at his disappointment, he aimed a blow at Tony with the long stick, as his boat shot past.

Tony was beyond his reach; he leaned over the gunwale of the boat in a vain attempt to accomplish his malignant purpose. But in doing so, he lost his foothold, and was precipitated head foremost into the lake !

He disappeared beneath the dark surface of the water, and his boat passed over the spot. The Zephyr, impelled backward by the vigorous strokes of her crew, was several rods from the place before the club fully realized the nature of the unfortunate occurrence.

The Thunderbolt was much nearer the place where
Tim had disappeared than the Zephyr; but her crew
seemed to be utterly paralyzed by the event, and
unable to render the slightest assistance.   One of
the Bunkers took the helm, and endeavored to rally
his companions; but in their confusion they were
incapable of handling their oars; some pulled one
way, and some another, and instead of urging the
boat ahead, they only turned it round in a circle.

"Stop her!" shouted Frank, as soon as he discovered the accident.   "Pull!   Tim Bunker has
fallen overboard!"

The crew, though affected to some extent as the
Bunkers were, used their oars with skill and energy.
The presence of mind which Frank displayed inspired
them with courage, and the Zephyr darted forward
towards the spot where Tim had gone down.

"There he is!" exclaimed Frank, with frantic
earnestness; "pull with all your might!"

"Help!   Save me!" cried Tim, as he rose to the
surface.

The boats were both several rods distant from
him.   He did not swim, but seemed to struggle

with all his strength, apparently with a spasmodic effort, as though he had entirely lost his self-control.

"Pull!" shouted Frank, again. "Tony, stand ready with your boathook."

But Tim struggled only for an instant on the surface, and then went down again.

"Steady," said Frank, as the Zephyr approached the spot. "That will do; back her!"

The boat, under the skilful management of the resolute young coxswain, lost her headway, and lay motionless on the water near the spot where Tim had last appeared.

"Do you see him, Tony?"

"No."

"Fred, forward with this boathook," continued Frank.

Fred took the boathook, and went forward to the bow of the Zephyr.

"There he is!" exclaimed Tony, as he caught a sight of the drowning boy beneath the surface.

Fred dropped his boathook down into the water with the intention of fastening it into his clothes.

" He sinks again ! " cried Tony, throwing off his jacket and shoes.

Before any of the crew could fully understand his purpose, so quick were his movements, he dove from the bow of the boat deep down into the water.

The boys held their breath in the intensity of their feelings. One or two of them had dropped their oar, and were leaving their places.

" Keep your places, and hold on to your oars ! " said Frank, sternly. " Henry Calrow, take the other boathook."

" Back her a little — one stroke," said Fred Harper. " We are passing over the spot."

Frank ordered the boat back, as desired.

" Here they rise ! Tony has him ! " exclaimed Fred, as he hooked into Tim's clothes. " Grasp the other boathook, Tony."

Tim was drawn into the boat, apparently dead.

Tony was so exhausted that he could not speak, and sank into the bottom.

" Pull ! " said Frank, heading the Zephyr towards Rippleton.

The sad event had been observed from the shore

and before the arrival of the club boat quite a number of persons had collected. Scarcely a minute elapsed before the Zephyr touched the bank, and the lifeless body of Tim Bunker was taken out and conveyed to the nearest house.

"How do you feel, Tony?" asked Frank, lifting the noble little fellow from his position.

"Badly, Frank; I want to go home," replied he, faintly.

Among other persons who had gathered on the shore of the lake was one of the physicians of Rippleton. He followed the party that conveyed Tim into the house, and applied himself vigorously to the means of restoring him. It was a long time before there were any signs of life, and the people in the mean time believed him dead.

While Dr. Allen was at work over Tim, Fred Harper came to request his assistance for Tony. Fortunately Dr. Davis, another physician, arrived at this moment, and accompanied him to the boat.

"What ails him, Dr. Davis?" asked Frank, alarmed by the illness of his friend.

"Exhaustion and excitement have affected him."

18

" Is it any thing serious ? "

" I think not. We must get his wet clothes off, and put him to bed."

" Will you go home with him ? We will row you up and back again."

The physician was very willing to go, and the boat put off. The club pulled with all their strength, and the distance to Tony's house was accomplished in a very few moments. Mrs. Weston was greatly alarmed when Tony was brought in, but the doctor assured her it was nothing serious. He was put to bed, the doctor prescribed for him, and when the boys were ready to leave, they had the satisfaction of knowing that the patient was much better.

When they reached Rippleton, they found that Tim had been restored, and conveyed to his father's house. Captain Sedley came in the last train, and the boys rowed him home.

CHAPTER XVII.

TIM BUNKER.

CAPTAIN SEDLEY was much disturbed by the painful event which had occurred, and though the club were entirely free from blame, he could not but question the expediency of continuing the organization. The malicious spirit of Tim Bunker had been the cause of his misfortune. People thought he was lucky to escape with his life, and that it would be a lesson he would remember a great many years.

Tony's praises were upon every body's lips. He had saved the life of his enemy, had plunged in at the risk of his own, to rescue one who had been intent upon his injury. It was a noble and a Christian deed, so the good men and women said, while others declared, if they had been in Tony's place, they would have let him drown.

The noble deed was appreciated, and the day after the event, a subscription paper was opened at the

Rippleton Bank for Tony's benefit. Before night over a hundred dollars were collected, which the cashier presented to him, as he lay upon his bed, sick from the effects of his exertions.

The crew of the boat club were very highly commended for their efficient labors on the occasion. If Frank had displayed less courage and address, or the discipline of the club had been less efficient, Tim must certainly have been drowned. This fact was rendered the more apparent by the contrast between the conduct of the crew of the Zephyr and that of the Thunderbolt. With all their exertion, on account of their want of discipline, the latter had been unable even to reach the spot until the former had received Tim on board.

All the sympathies of the people were with the boat club. Nobody pitied Tim; for he was a quarrelsome, disagreeable boy, and had nearly lost his life in his attempt to gratify his malicious spite against his noble and generous deliverer.

In a few days, Tony, who had suffered more from the shock than Tim, was able to go out again. He was every where received with enthusiasm, and the first time the Zephyr visited Rippleton after the accident, people seemed determined to make a little lion of him.

Captain Sedley's attention was now directed to the trial of Tony, which would take place in a few days, and he was exceedingly desirous of ascertaining how Tim was affected towards him since the rescue. But the Thunderbolt had been laid up at Joe Braman's landing, and the Bunkers appeared to be dispersed and separated since the accident. Captain Sedley did not find their leader for several days, but at last he made a visit to his father's house before Tim got up.

He was very desirous of avoiding him, and when his mother went up stairs and told him who had come, he put on his clothes, and slipped out of the house by the back door. Captain Sedley happened to see him, however, as he was skulking off through the garden.

"Tim," said he, running after him.

The leader of the Bunkers did not dare to run away from such an influential person as Captain Sedley, and turning. he doggedly approached him.

"Tim, I want to see you about the trial, which, you know, takes place in a few days."

"I don't know nothin' about it."

"You don't?" said Captain Sedley.

"No, I don't;" and Tim, fixing his eyes upon the ground, amused himself by kicking a hole in the soil with his foot.

"Don't you know any thing about the wallet, or the money that was in it?"

"No, I don't."

"Just think a moment."

"Don't want to think; I don't know nothin' about it," replied Tim, sulkily.

"Tony is accused of the crime, and you know what a terrible thing it would be to have an innocent person suffer."

"I 'spose it would."

"You know Tony saved your life."

"So I needn't be evidence against him," growled Tim.

Captain Sedley was astonished at his want of even the commonest feeling of gratitude.

"If that had been his motive, he would have let you drown."

"I wonder he didn't."

"Tim, you are utterly hardened in iniquity."

"No, I ain't."

"You have no gratitude towards your deliverer."

"Yes, I have ; I am much obliged to him for what he done, and when I see him, I'll tell him so."

"You do not *seem* in the least obliged to him."

"I am ; and besides, the folks gave him over a hundred dollars for what he done. I should like to jump in after a dozen on the same terms."

"You have nothing to say about the trial then, have you, Tim ? "

"Don't know nothin' about it. All I can say is, I saw him stickin' somethin' into his pocket."

"You bought the boat in which you have been sailing on the lake."

"No, I didn't ; it is Joe Braman's," replied Tim, stoutly.

"Did you tell the boys that you gave him ten dollars for it ? "

"No, I didn't."

"And that you paid five dollars for having it fitted up?"

"I was only joking — tryin' to sell 'em," answered Tim, attempting to smile and look funny.

"That was it, was it?"

"That's all."

"And you have not paid Joe Braman any money?"

"Not a cent."

"Tim," said Captain Sedley, sternly, "people think that you stole the wallet."

"Me! I hope to die if I did!"

"That you took some of the money out, and then put it into Tony's pocket, so as to fasten the guilt on him."

"No such thing!"

"Just consider, Tim. If you did, you had better confess it."

"I didn't."

"Only think that Tony saved your life."

"I've nothin' against him."

"But you ought to be for him. If you have injured him in this matter, people will think a great deal better of you, if you confess it, and ask his forgiveness, whatever the consequences may be to yourself."

" I hain't injured him."

" If you are the guilty one, it will certainly come out at the trial."

" I ain't ; I don't know nothin' about the wallet. I'm sure I didn't take it — I hope to die if I did ! "

" Very well, Tim ; if you have made up your mind not to confess it, I have nothing more to say."

" I ain't a going to confess it when I didn't do it," said Tim, stoutly.

" But you did do it, Tim."

" No, I didn't nuther."

" I am surprised at your hardihood. Tony saved your life at the peril of his own, and yet you are willing to see him convicted of a crime which you committed yourself."

" Who says I did ? " said Tim, not a little confused by the directness with which Captain Sedley spoke to him.

" I say it, Tim. Once more, will you free Tony from the charge by telling the truth ? "

" I have told the truth."

" No, you haven't, Tim.   Will you confess the crime, and save Tony ? "

" No, I won't; I didn't do it."

" Very well," replied Captain Sedley, as he left the young reprobate.

Tim did not know what to make of it. Why Captain Sedley should lay it to him, he could not tell, unless it was on account of what he had said to Fred Harper about buying the Thunderbolt. He was uneasy, and spent the forenoon in wandering about the woods back of his father's house. He felt as though something was going to happen, though he could not ell precisely what.

He had eaten no breakfast, and at noon he was driven home by hunger. But he had scarcely seated himself at the dinner table before a knock was heard at the door.

" Go to the door, Tim," said his father.

" I don't want to go," answered Tim, with a whine.

A kind of dread had taken possession of him since his interview with Captain Sedley in the morning, and every noise he heard seemed to foretell "that something" he was persuaded was about to occur.

"Go, this minute!" said his father, sternly.

"Don't want to."

"But you shall."

Tim, finding there was no escape, rose, and went to the door. To his consternation he beheld Mr. Headley, the constable! He felt as though he should drop through the floor. His heart beat so violently that he could hardly stand up.

"I want you, Tim," said Mr. Headley.

"Me!" gasped Tim.

"Get your cap, and come along."

"What for?"

"I'll tell you when you get to the jail."

Tim drew a long breath, and went back for his cap.

"Who is it, Tim?" asked his father.

But Tim made no reply, and instead of returning to the front door, he took his cap and sneaked out through the back room. The woods were close by, and the hope of escaping inspired him with new courage. Throwing open the back door, he rushed out.

"So, so! my fine fellow!" exclaimed the constable, who stood before the door, and into whose arms he had thrown himself as he leaped down the doorsteps. "This is your plan, is it? We'll give you the ruffles, then."

So saying, Mr. Headley took a pair of handcuffs from his pocket, and fastened them upon Tim's wrists.

"I didn't steal the wallet," cried Tim, lustily, as he struggled to get away.

"You must come with me," replied the constable, holding him fast.

Tim's father and mother came to the door, as Mr Headley marched him off.

CHAPTER XVIII.

TONY'S TRIAL.

JOE BRAMAN was arrested on the same day, and committed to the Rippleton jail. It was understood that suspicions were fastened upon him, though the precise nature of the testimony against him had not yet been made public. His examination, as well as that of Tim Bunker, was postponed until after the trial of Tony, which had been appointed, in consideration of the circumstances, for the following day.

Captain Sedley had been very active in obtaining evidence, but he was so cautious that the people of Rippleton could not ascertain what he was doing.

The morning of the trial came. The members of the boat club were all anxious to attend, and Captain Sedley had consented that they should go to the village in the Zephyr, taking Uncle Ben with them as boat keeper.

At nine o'clock the club had all assembled in the boat house, and had put on their uniform.

"Keep your spirits up, Tony," said Fred. "It will all come out right."

"I hope so," replied Tony, rather sadly. "I am innocent, and all I ask is justice."

"My father is very sure you will be cleared," added Frank; "but whether you are or not, we are all very certain of your innocence."

"Thank you; you have been very kind to me and my mother," answered Tony, the tears gathering in his eyes as he spoke. "I heard last evening what you did the night before the fourth of July."

"Never mind that, Tony; we all like you. You are a noble fellow;" and Frank grasped the hand of his friend.

"I don't know as I ought to wear this uniform to-day," continued Tony, trying to smile through his tears.

"Why not, Tony."

"I don't want to disgrace the club."

"Disgrace us, Tony! I am sure there is not a

fellow in the club that does not feel honored by having you belong."

" Think of your uniform on the back of a felon. If found guilty, I shall be sent to the house of correction."

" But you won't be, Tony. Tim and Joe Braman have been arrested, and you may be sure there has been some evidence found to fasten it upon them."

" Perhaps so ; at least, I am innocent, and I shall be just as innocent in the house of correction as in the open air. But I don't want to disgrace the club."

" I talked with father about the • uniform last night. He thought we had better not wear it, because it would look so odd in the court house ; but I told him we wanted to wear it, so as to show that you were one of us."

" You are very kind, Frank," replied Tony, grasping his hand.

" Time you were off, boys," said Uncle Ben.

" Take your places," continued Frank.

The members of the club seemed to feel that they were not going on a pleasure excursion, and there was hardly a smile to be seen on their faces. They were quiet, and very orderly, and moved slowly and with a good deal of dignity into the boat.

The Zephyr backed out of her berth, and the oars fell into the water.

"Pull," said Frank, as he laid the course of the boat towards Rippleton. "We will not hoist our flags going down."

The crew pulled steadily, and not a word was spoken on the way. Every member was thinking of poor Tony, and every one was hoping and believing that he would be triumphantly acquitted.

On their arrival at Rippleton, Frank formed them in procession, two by two, and marched up to the court house. More than once, as they passed through the streets, the people, recognizing Tony, lustily cheered him. Since the rescue of Tim Bunker, he had been a hero in the village. His misfortunes, added to his noble, generous character, excited all the sympathies of the people.

When they reached the court house, the sheriff, as a special mark of consideration, conducted them to seats where they could see and hear all that was bone and said.

Squire Benson was at the table, and the jury were in their seats, but the court had not yet come in. Captain Sedley and Mrs. Weston had chairs by the side of Tony's counsel, and were engaged in an earnest conversation with him.

" Where shall I stay ? " asked Tony of the sheriff.

" I suppose you must take your place in the dock," replied the official.

" I am ready."

There was a sudden silence in the room, as the sheriff conducted the little prisoner to the box appropriated to the criminals. The audience felt deeply for him, and his poor mother burst into tears.

The judge took his seat on the bench, and the crier opened the court. The indictment was read, and Tony, in a firm, and even cheerful tone, pleaded "not guilty."

The county attorney made his opening address, and the witnesses for the prosecution were sworn. These consisted of Farmer Whipple, Mr. Headley, Charles Hardy, Frank Sedley, and Tim Bunker, the latter of whom was brought into court by the constable.

The testimony was substantially the same as at the examination. It was proved that Tony was in the woodhouse, had seen the wallet, and left his companions to find Farmer Whipple; that he had been seen to put something into his pocket, and finally that the lost property had been found upon him.

It was a clear case, and when they came to the end of the evidence, Mrs. Weston sobbed bitterly.

"Be comforted, madam, your son shall be proved innocent in a few moments," said Squire Benson.

The cross examination of Tim Bunker was very long and very severe, and though he still adhered to the story he had told at the examination, he was confused, stammered a great deal, and tried to be saucy to the lawyer. His statements were so contradictory at times, that a general disposition to laugh pervaded the minds of the audience. At these times, when he so grossly crossed himself, Squire Benson looked significantly at the jury, as though to invite their special attention to the discrepancies.

Tony's counsel then opened the case for the defence. His address was very short, but very pointed and forcible.

The first witness was Mr. Doolittle, the store-keeper, who testified to the facts concerning the twenty dollar bill.

"Is that the bill you marked?" asked the lawyer, handing him a bank note.

"It is," replied the witness, after examining it.

"You are willing to swear that is the bill?"

"I am."

"Please state to the court and jury the means by which you identify it."

The witness exhibited his shop card upon the back of it, and pointed out several other peculiarities, which he had observed while stamping it.

"Mr. Stevens," said the lawyer. "That will do, Mr. Doolittle."

The person called took the stand. He was a stranger in Rippleton, and the audience wondered what he could possibly know about it.

"Your business, Mr. Stevens?" continued the lawyer, scratching furiously with his pen.

"I keep a hardware store in Boston."

"Did you ever see this bill?" and Squire Benson handed him the bank note.

" I have."

" State, if you please, what you know about it."

" It was given to me in payment for a fowling piece."

" When ? "

The witness gave the date.

" Can you swear to the bill ? "

" I can ; I wrote my name and the day of the month on it at the time ; here they are."

" Indeed ! how happened you to do that ? "

" I did it at the request of the gentleman who sits by your side ; " and the witness pointed to Captain Sedley.

" Who was the person that gave you the bill ? "

" I do not know his name."

" Could you identify him ? "

" I could."

Squire Benson requested the court to have Joe Braman summoned as a witness in the case, and after a short delay, he was brought in by an officer.

" Was that the person ? "

" It was."

" You are sure ? "

" I noticed the scar on his cheek," replied the witness, " and I should not be likely to mistake such a person as that for another."

The audience smiled at this sally. Joe Braman was in truth an oddity in his personal appearance, and the remark of the witness seemed to have a peculiar force.

" That is all, Mr. Stevens; the witness is yours, Mr. Prescott," said Squire Benson, turning to the county attorney.

But Mr. Prescott asked him no questions.

" Joseph Braman, take the stand," continued Tony's lawyer.

Joe seemed bewildered by the circumstances that surrounded him, and gazed vacantly at the judge and jury. He was a dull, stupid fellow, and did not readily comprehend his position.

He was sworn, and after the judge had reminded him that he need not criminate himself, Squire Benson proceeded with the examination.

" You bought a gun of the last witness, did you not ? " asked he.

" Yes, sir," replied Joe, scarcely knowing whether he was on trial himself or not.

" You gave him a twenty dollar bill, did you not ? "

" You are suggesting his answers," interposed the county attorney.

" What did you give him in payment ? "

" I gin him a twenty dollar bill," replied Joe, promptly.

" This was the bill, wasn't it ? "

" I pray your honor's judgment," said the county attorney, with a smile. " My learned brother answers the question, and then puts it."

" Put the question fairly, Mr. Benson," added the judge.

" Was this the bill ? " said the lawyer, handing the witness the twenty dollar note.

" I rather guess it was."

" You guess !   Don't you know ? " said Mr. Benson, with severity in his tone and manner.

" Yes, sir, it was," answered Joe, startled by the questioner's sharp words.

' How do you know ? "

" I see'd this 'ere mark on't," replied the witness, pointing to Mr. Doolittle's shop card.

" Now, Mr. Braman," continued Squire Benson, suddenly softening his tone, and assuming a pleasant smile, " Where did you get this bill ? "

" *Tim Bunker gin it to me.*"

The reply of Joe produced a great sensation in the court room.

" I told you so ! " whispered Charles Hardy to Frank.

There was a smile of triumph on the face of Tony, when, at this point, all eyes were turned to him.

" It's a lie ! " groaned Tim, his face as white as a sheet.

" Did he tell you where he got it ? " continued Mr. Benson, in an apparently indifferent tone.

" You need not criminate yourself," interposed the judge.

" He told me all about it," replied Joe, suddenly brushing up his wits.

" You needn't wink at me, Tim ; I'm goin' to blow the whole thing," continued he, shaking his head at the crestfallen Bunker. "You was fool enough to tell on't yourself."

"He told you that he stole it?" asked Squire Benson.

"No; he said he found it," and the witness pro-ceeded to relate all the particulars of the affair.

It appeared from his story that Tim had taken the wallet, abstracted thirty dollars of the money, and then, when school was about to be dismissed, had thrust the wallet into the prisoner's pocket.

Tony had not discovered the wallet. He had eaten his dinner and gone immediately into the garden, where he had pulled off his coat, and com-menced picking the currants. Tim's plan had worked better than he expected it would, for he supposed that Tony would find it in his pocket, and be ac-cused of abstracting the thirty dollars.

The jury gave in their verdict of not guilty, with-out leaving their seats. As they did so, a gentle-man, with a very long beard and mustache, rose and clapped his hands with great violence. His example was followed by a large portion of the audience, and the sheriff had much trouble in restoring order.

CHAPTER XIX.

THE STRANGER.

THE officer immediately released the prisoner from his confinement, and Tony sprang into the waiting arms of his mother.

"Bless you, my boy!" she exclaimed, as the tears rolled down her cheeks. "I knew you were innocent!"

"My carriage waits for you, Mrs. Weston," said Captain Sedley, after he had cordially shaken the hand of Squire Benson.

The widow thanked the lawyer for his good service, and the party withdrew from the court room. In the street, amid the cheers of the multitude, the boat club formed their lines, and marched down to the lake.

When they reached the Zephyr, they found her in charge of one of the men who worked on the farm of Captain Sedley.

" Where is Uncle Ben ? " asked Frank.

" Gone home," replied the man.

" What for ? "

" I don't know."

" Take your places," said Frank.

Just as the oars were dipping, they were hailed from the shore.

" Boat, ahoy," said a stranger on the bank.

Frank looked, and discovered the gentleman who had commenced the applause in the court room. He was well dressed, wore a massive gold chain, and appeared to be in affluent circumstances, if one might judge from appearances. His face — that portion of it which was not covered by his long black beard — was very dark, and apparently he had just returned from a tropical climate.

The coxswain ordered the crew to cease rowing.

" Can you tell me how I shall get to the house of John Weston, up the lake ? " inquired the stranger.

" John Weston is not living," replied Frank.

" Not living ! " replied the stranger, with a sudden start.   " Is Mrs. Weston living ? "

" She is."

" She is my mother," added Tony.

" We are going up there now, and if you choose we will row you up."

" Thank you," replied the stranger, as he seated himself by Frank's side.

Tony gazed at him with intense earnestness. The face looked natural to him, but he could not think where he had seen it before.

" Pull," said Frank.

" You have a beautiful boat."

" She is a very fine boat.* I saw you at the trial, did I not ? " asked Frank, looking with interest at his companion.

" I was there ; it ended very happily."

" Just as we knew it would end," added Charles Hardy.

" It was a villanous conspiracy; and I should like the pleasure of thrashing that Tim Bunker," continued the stranger, with a great deal of feeling.

" You seemed to be much interested in the trial."

" More deeply than any other could be."

" Except his mother," said Frank.

" You are right, except his mother ; " and the

gentleman looked very sad, and wiped a tear from his eye.

The boat was now approaching the vicinity of Centre Island.

" This is Captain Sedley's place," said the stranger

" Yes, sir."

" There comes the Sylph, Frank," shouted Fred Harper.

" Uncle Ben is up to something, I suspect."

" What do you suppose it is ? "

Before Frank could venture an opinion, a mass of smoke rose from the bows of the Sylph, and the mimic roar of a little cannon was heard.

" Hurrah ! Tony, he is firing a salute in honor of the verdict," cried Charles.

" Three cheers for Tony Weston," shouted Frank.
" One ! "

" Hurrah ! "

" Two ! "

" Hurrah ! "

" Three ! "

" Hurrah ! "

The stranger joined lustily in the cheers, and when

tney had finished, Uncle Ben fired again. When the Zephyr came alongside the Sylph, the veteran congratulated the little hero of the day on his escape from the snares of his foes.

"You are a good boy, and I wish I had a bigger gun. You desarve a salute from a forty-two pounder," said Uncle Ben, as he rammed down the charge for another gun.

"Thank you, Uncle Ben, that gun is big enough for so small a boy as I am."

The Zephyr continued on her course to the widow Weston's, followed by the Sylph, the old sailor saluting all the way.

The party landed, and marched up to the house, followed by the stranger. Tony embraced his sister and his little brother, and with tears of joy told them that he was acquitted. Mrs. Weston and Captain Sedley had not yet arrived.

In half an hour they came. Mrs. Weston welcomed her guests, and among them the stranger.

"I don't know you, sir, but you are welcome to my poor cottage," said she, with a courtesy.

"Thank you, ma'am. I have just come from

20 *

California. I believe you had a son who went out there."

"I did. Poor George! I suppose he is dead," answered the widow, wiping a tear from her eye.

"I come to tell you about him, ma'am."

"Then he is dead!"

"No; he is alive and well."

"Heaven bless you for the news!" ejaculated the poor woman.

It was indeed a day of gladness to her.

"He is coming home soon."

"I am glad to hear it. Where has he been?"

"He has been at the mines."

"I haven't heard a word from him since he first reached San Francisco."

"He has written several times; but the means of communication with San Francisco and the diggings were very uncertain. I suppose his letters miscarried."

"But tell me about him. Has his health been good?"

"Very good; and he has been remarkably lucky.

Folks say he has made over a hundred thousand
dollars digging and trading."

" Indeed ! I am so glad ! "

" I suppose you don't remember me, do you ? "
asked the stranger.

The widow looked at him sharply.

" You have got such a sight of hair on your face,
that I declare I do not," said the widow, laughing.

" You don't ? "

The gentleman spoke these words in a different
tone of voice — so different that the widow started
back in astonishment.

" Have I altered so much, mother ? "

" George ! O George ! " exclaimed the widow,
as she folded her lost son in her arms.

They both wept in each other's embrace.

" Heaven be praised, you have returned ! " cried
the widow.

" And my father is dead ? " said George Weston
sadly.

" Yes, George, you have no father now."

The young man trembled with emotion.

"I had hoped to smooth the last years of his life; but God's will be done."

"Amen!" said the widow, solemnly, as she wiped her eyes.

"Tony, my brother, come here," said George, as he shook the hand of the little hero. "You cannot think how badly I felt this morning, when, on my arrival at Rippleton, I heard that you were to be tried for stealing. If it had not been for our mother, I think I should have fled from the place without making myself known."

"But, George, I was innocent."

"I know it, Tony, and I was the happiest man in the court house, when I heard that Joe Braman confess the truth."

"And, George," interrupted Mrs. Weston, "you must join with me in thanking Captain Sedley here for all he has done for poor Tony. I am sure, if it had not been for him, he would have been found guilty."

George Weston took the hand of Captain Sedley, and in fit terms expressed his gratitude.

"And we have to thank him for a thousand other

favors since your poor father's death. I don't know what would have become of us without him."

George renewed his thanks, and called down the blessing of Heaven on the benefactor of his mother.

"Come, boys, we had better go," said Captain Sedley.

The boat club withdrew, with the exception of Tony.

"Mrs. Weston, I shall be happy to see you and all your family at my house at tea this evening," continued Captain Sedley.

"Thank you, sir; we shall certainly come," replied the widow.

"And, Captain Sedley, my mother shall soon have a house to which she can invite her friends," said George Weston, with a smile.

The little front room of the widow Weston's cottage was the scene of a joyful reunion on that eventful day. George related his adventures to his mother, and shed many a tear when he heard her tell of the trials through which she had passed during his absence. The future was still open to him, and he determined to fill it with joys for her, which should,

in some measure, compensate her for the sorrow and
suffering of the past; for George regarded poverty
and want as misery, and did not see how his mother
could have been contented, as she professed to have
been.

After dinner the site for a new house was selected,
plans were matured for sending Mary to the Rippleton Academy, and Tony was to be kept at the gram-
mar school till he was qualified for the high school.

About four o'clock, when all these things had been
fully discussed, George and Tony walked down to
the banks of the lake.

" There comes the Zephyr," said the latter. " We
have fine times in her, George, I can tell you."

" Whose boat is she ? "

" Frank Sedley's ; his father gave it to him."

" You must have one, Tony."

" Me ! "

" Yes ; I am able to give you one, and when I go
to the city I will order one built."

" How liberal you are, George ! "

" You are a good boy, Tony ; and a good boy de-
serves every thing it is proper for him to have."

" But we don't need another. We have just as good times in the Zephyr as though each owned a share in her. There is nothing mean about Frank Sedley, I can tell you!" said Tony, with enthusiasm.

" He seems to be a very fine little fellow," added George.

" That he is; why, only last fourth of July he gave mother all the money he had saved for the occasion, instead of spending it. What do you say to that?"

" That was noble. My poor mother! Was she indeed reduced to such extremity as that!"

" She didn't want it; but he would give it to her, and she bought new dresses for herself and Mary with it."

" It was very generous, and he shall lose nothing by it."

" Charley Hardy did the same, and both of them staid at home on the fourth."

" They shall be rewarded. But the new boat, Tony?"

" I don't think we need another."

" If you had another you could race a little, and manœuvre together."

" That would be nice, wouldn't it ? "

" I will speak with Captain Sedley about it. Here comes the boat."

" We have come to row you up to my father's," said the coxswain.

" Thank you, Frank," replied George. " We shall be very happy to accompany you."

Mrs. Weston and Mary were all ready, and the party seated themselves in the stern sheets of the Zephyr. On their way down the lake, the scheme of having another club boat was discussed and fully matured.

" What will you call her, Tony ? " asked Charles.

" I don't know," said Tony, musing. " What do you think of the Butterfly ? "

" Capital ! " exclaimed George.

The matter was all arranged, and the party soon reached the boat house, and spent a pleasant evening in the hospitable mansion of Captain Sedley.

CHAPTER XX.

CONCLUSION.

THE first two weeks of the organization of the boat club passed away, and the members were assembled in Zephyr Hall to elect a coxswain. According to the constitution, Frank's term of office had expired.

" Whom do you intend to vote for, Fred ? " asked Charles Hardy, who appeared to be very anxious about the election.

" I don't know ; I haven't decided yet," replied Fred Harper. " You know what Captain Sedley said the other day about it."

" Yes, but if I have got to vote, I want to get my mind made up. I don't see what harm there can be in talking about it a little."

" He said he did not want any electioneering about the officers — 'log rolling,' my father calls it."

" Of course not," replied Charles, demurely.

21

" The best fellow ought to get the office," said Fred, slyly.

" Of course, but who is the best fellow ? That's the question. We ought to talk it over among ourselves a little."

" What good would that do ? "

" Each fellow would know whom the others were going to vote for."

" That would not help him to ascertain who would make the best coxswain."

" But it would help towards making a choice."

" There will be a choice fast enough."

" I don't believe it. If there is no nomination and no understanding about the matter beforehand, every fellow will vote for a different person. You see if there are not a dozen different ones voted for."

" We can try it over again, then," said Fred, with a laugh.

" I shall vote for you, and perhaps you will vote for me."

" *Perhaps* I shall."

" And that is the way it will be all through the club."

"Charley, what do you say to giving Frank a re-election?" said Fred, with sudden energy, while the mischief seemed to beam from his eyes.

"Well, I don't know," replied Charles, looking intently at the floor.

"Frank has made a good coxswain; there is no rubbing that out."

"Very good," said Charles, feebly.

"If it hadn't been for him, Tim Bunker would have been drowned that time."

"Couldn't another fellow have done the same that he did?"

"Yes, if he had had the presence of mind and the energy of character which Frank has."

"You could have done it, Fred."

"I don't know about that."

"You hauled him in with the boathook."

"Yes, but I only did what Frank told me to do. Look at the Bunkers; they didn't even reach the spot till we had got him on board the Zephyr."

"I should not have been afraid but that I could have managed the boat as well as Frank did."

"I don't know but you could, Charley."

" I am pretty sure I could."

" Perhaps you will be elected the next coxswain, Charley," continued Fred ; and there was a slight twinkle in his mischievous eye.

" No ! O, no ! I'm sure *I* don't want to be coxswain."

" You don't ! "

" No ; I never thought of such a thing."

" Didn't ? "

" I'm sure I never did."

· Then I will tell the fellows, so that they needn't throw, their votes away upon you," said Fred, roguishly.

" Well, as to that, of course I should serve if chosen.   I want to do just what the fellows want to have me."

" They don't want you to be coxswain if you don't wish to be, because there are enough of them who do desire the office."

" Well, I don't exactly want it, but —— "

Charles suddenly paused.

" But what, Charley ? "·

" I want the club should have the best officer we can get."

Fred laughed heartily.

" I want the office, Charley ; I should like it first rate," continued he ; " but I don't much expect to get it, and am perfectly willing to abide the decision of the club. Majority rules."

" Order," said Frank Sedley, rapping on the table.

The boys all took their chairs, and Frank stated the business of the meeting, which was to elect a coxswain for the next two weeks.

" Our director will be with us in a moment," continued he, " and has something to say before we proceed with the election."

" Here he comes," said Fred.

" Mr. Chairman, and members of the Zephyr Boat Club," began Captain Sedley, with a smile on his benevolent features, " you remember I cautioned you a week ago not to talk about this election. I presume you have observed my request. I had strong reasons for doing so. In the first place, I do not wish to have any unpleasant feelings excited by these elections ; and in the second place, I wish you to

21 *

learn the first duty of a republican citizen — to cast
an independent vote.   Among boys, as among men,
there is often one or more who wield an influence
over others — an influence which is not always directed by truth and justice.   One, by his mental
power or social position, controls others.   They follow his example without always inquiring whether it
is good or bad.   I want you to think for yourselves;
to make up your minds, without any assistance from
others, in regard to the fitness of the person for
whom you vote.   I desire each of you to deposit
his ballot in the box, without communication with
others — without telling them, or letting them know
by any means, for whom you vote.   Now the box is
ready, and you may separate to prepare your votes.
The poll shall be kept open ten minutes."

Some of the boys went out into the boat room,
and others out of doors.   They were all very particular to comply to the letter with Captain Sedley's
request.   The ballot box was kept closed, so that no
one could read the names on the votes, and only
opened enough to admit the slip of paper.

Before the ten minutes had expired the members

were all in their seats. There was a great deal of interest manifested in the result, and not a little anxiety was visible in the expression of several faces — that of Charles Hardy in particular.

" Have you all voted ? " said Frank. " I declare the poll closed."

" I will count the votes," interposed Captain Sedley, " so as to give you all the benefit of the excitement."

Taking the box in his hand, he went out in the boat room.

" Who do you think has got it ? " whispered Charles to Fred Harper.

" I have no idea ; I only know whom I vote for."

" Whom ? "

" What would you give to know ? "

" Yourself ? "

" Indeed, I did not ! " replied Fred, indignantly.

" There would be no harm in it if you did, would there ? "

" No harm ? It would only amount to saying, ' I am the best fellow in the club.' "

" No, not that ; it would only be saying that **you** wanted the office."

" Rather more than that."

" But you said you did want it."

" I didn't vote for myself, any how.   But here comes Captain Sedley.   Hush ! "

" Here is the result, Frank," said the director, handing him the ballots and a little slip of paper on which he had written the names and number of votes.   " Read it."

There was a breathless silence when Frank rose, and every member exhibited the deepest interest in the proceedings.

" Whole number of votes, thirteen," the coxswain read from the paper.   " Necessary for a choice, seven. Charles Hardy has one ; Frederic Harper has one ; and Anthony Weston has eleven, and is elected coxswain of the club for the ensuing two weeks."

" Three cheers for Tony Weston ! " shouted Fred Harper, rising.   " One."

The cheers were given with hearty good will and emphasis.

" Mr. Chairman," said Charles, " I move we make the vote unanimous."

Charles had been reading the proceedings of a political nominating convention, where they make the nomination unanimous so as to show the unity of the party ; and his ideas were rather confused.

" Those in favor of Anthony Weston for coxswain the next two weeks, say 'Ay,' continued Frank.

" Ay ! "

" It is a unanimous vote. Tony, I am happy to resign my office to you, and I feel that it could not have been conferred upon a more worthy member," said Frank, leaving his arm chair.

" But, Mr. Chairman, I am clerk. I am very much obliged to the club for the honor," said Tony, blushing up to the eyes.

" You are coxswain, Tony, and the clerkship is vacant," added Captain Sedley. " The members of the club, without consultation with each other, have elected you — the most convincing evidence they could possibly give of the high esteem in which they hold you."

After some persuasion, Tony took the chair, and

Fred Harper was elected clerk. Frank took Tony's number, and the stroke oar was appropriated to him.

The business was finished, and the club proceeded to the boat room, to prepare for their first excursion under the new coxswain. After the meeting had broken up, there was considerable inquiry for the member who had voted for Charles Hardy; but he could not be found. Tony had voted for Fred Harper, and the conclusion that Charles had voted for himself was irresistible.

But Charles, in spite of his hypocritical character, was a well meaning boy. His desire to appear well, and to be "first and foremost," sometimes led him astray, and the discipline of the club finally worked a "great improvement in him." He was not elected coxswain that year, for on the first of November, the Zephyr was laid up for the winter. Fred Harper was elected after Tony, who served his term with credit to himself, and to the discipline of the club.

The Butterfly was not completed in season to be launched that year; but the following spring a second club was formed, and Tony was the first coxswain. During the winter the Zephyrs met regularly at their hall, for mutual improvement. At the suggestion of Fred Harper, a debating society was formed, and the members derived a great deal of pleasure, and obtained an excellent mental discipline, from their discussions.

To add to the interest of their meetings, George Weston gave them a number of familiar lectures on "California;" Captain Sedley on "Life on the Ocean;" and Mr. Hyde, the schoolmaster, on "Natural Philosophy and Chemistry." The boys declared they never enjoyed a winter so much; and certainly they derived a great deal of useful information from these pleasant meetings.

Tim Bunker and Joe Braman were tried at the next session of the court, — the former for stealing and the latter for receiving stolen property, — and sentenced to the house of correction.

George Weston's new house was completed before winter, and the family were nicely settled before the first snow came. The widow Weston was happy all day long in the presence of her children, and never ceased to thank God for all the blessings with which

her life had been crowned — the blessings of adver-
sity as well as those of prosperity.

The following spring the Butterfly was launched,
the new club organized, and the sports of the season
opened with a grand May day picnic and dance on
Centre Island. But I have not space to tell my
young readers how Mary Weston was made Queen
of May, how the Zephyr and the Butterfly raced up
and down the lake, and how the latter got beaten on
account of the inexperience of her crew. I have
told my story, and I leave the boat club, and all the
characters contented and happy in the enjoyment of
the many blessings that were showered upon them.